It Had to Be You

Anuj Tiwari is the author of the bestselling novel *Journey of Two Hearts*, a motivational speaker and an IT professional. His books are based on real life incidents that he jotted down over the years. He gives lectures at colleges and universities, and lives in Mumbai.

You can get in touch with him via Facebook at www.facebook.com/anujtiwari.official or email him at anujtiwari.official@gmail.com.

Praise for *Journey of Two Hearts*

'Pearls have come down on paper.'—*Amar Ujala*

'An unforgettable love story.'—*Afternoon*

It Had to Be You

Anuj Tiwari

RUPA

First published by
Rupa Publications India Pvt. Ltd 2014
7/16, Ansari Road, Daryaganj
New Delhi 110002

Sales Centres:

Allahabad Bengaluru Chennai
Hyderabad Jaipur Kathmandu
Kolkata Mumbai

ISBN: 978-81-291-3107-2

First impression 2014

10 9 8 7 6 5 4 3 2 1

The moral right of the author has been asserted.

Printed by Thomson Press India Ltd, Faridabad

To Pakhi's family
and my parents, who gave me the best quality of DNA
because I survived when everything seemed lost.

Loving someone is not tough,
But the real courage is to forget your loved one.
The way we met, we met for a reason.
We loved once, we lived once,
Then we got the reason to live for each other...forever.

Contents

I Didn't Have the Perfect Love

'Have you packed everything?' Mom asked. I knew she was suppressing tears but wasn't showing them. Mothers are like that.

'Yes,' I replied.

'Keep your medicines, take care of yourself and promise me this won't happen again.' She looked at me for an acknowledgment but it was hard to meet her expectations at times. I couldn't make any false promises to her and uttered a non-committal 'Hmm.'

'Listen to me…I'm trying to say something.' She pulled me in front of her and looked at me sternly.

'Mom, you know that is difficult, at least for me.' Just as I said this, dad entered the room—just the person I didn't want to discuss these things with.

'What's difficult? You're going away from home; you've just been released from the hospital. Wasn't that more difficult—staying at the hospital for six months to treat depression? Anuj, this is the time to concentrate on your life and it's up to you to utilize this opportunity or waste it away,' Dad said.

His words hurt me deeply.

I've lost everything in the last few months—my friends, my happiness and my parents' trust. I've caused my family so much pain. But even after all this, will she come back into my life? I thought. I didn't say anything to dad, however, who understood, patted my shoulder and left the room.

'She won't come back into your life, you know that. Why are you wasting your life away for her?' Mom asked, trying to reason with me.

'Mom, I can't promise you that, and you know that very well. We've discussed it several times now.' I zipped up the bag.

The next day I was to leave for Mumbai to start a job with a prominent MNC. I didn't really want to leave home but the time had come for me to take on more responsibilities. I knew that my loneliness was going to make my life hell, though. Suddenly, I couldn't handle my frustration in any longer. I threw my small carry bag in the corner and sat on the bed. Mom understood. She was the one who trusted me most and had high hopes for me. She came and sat next to me.

'Anuj, stop it now. That's enough. I don't want to repeat these things over and over. We both know that Pakhi isn't with you— in fact, you don't even know where she is. We've suffered a lot because of her. Why're you still pining for someone who never cared about you? What's happened to you? Don't you love your mother? Don't you care about your family?' she cried as she reached out to hug me.

The purest love in the universe is the love of a mother. And that made me more emotional when I recalled that she had been softly crying the previous night when I had woken up to have water. The thought of my leaving was clearly painful for her.

With those unanswered questions, I left early next morning for Mumbai. Though I didn't cry in front of them when she and dad came to drop me off at the railway station, we knew how we all felt for each other. Sometimes we love our family so much that we don't have the courage to express it. I wanted to hug them but couldn't gather the courage as everything was happening for the first time. I broke down on the train, though, and cried till I reached Mumbai the next morning.

There, I searched in vain for at least one person to share my pain with. I forgot how to treat people, how to talk to them and how to make friends. Time changed people, and my life had changed completely.

The video I had made for her was still in that hidden folder, and it still made me cry. I was still alive; I could breathe, I could eat, I could walk and talk, but when I breathed, there was no fragrance in the air; when I ate, I couldn't taste anything; when I walked, my heart wasn't in it. Days and nights seemed endless. All my smiles were temporary, superficial. I cursed my destiny.

Now there were no romantic messages on my phone; only a few songs of her choice remained. I stopped replying to any messages from my friends, stopped picking up calls. I started keeping my cell phone on silent; eventually, I stopped carrying it altogether. After all, there was no one left to call me. For several days, I forgot to wash my clothes, polish my shoes, and comb my hair. I started skipping dinner as I lost my appetite, and if my friends forced me to eat with them, I vomited in the middle of the night. I lost kilos of weight in six months. All I ate were the tablets prescribed to keep my blood pressure normal and cure my depression.

I started looking unhealthy, as well. Soon, people started ignoring me—nobody liked to sit with me or talk to me. I loved to sleep but now I started hating the night. Every morning, the memory of her made me cry, and that became a part of my life.

I was still on my medication, a patient of depression, and a victim of love. Weeks passed and then...

Punjabi Girls Always Rock

'At what time are you leaving tomorrow?' Vishal asked me in his adenoidal voice, sitting on the bed.

'Early morning at 5 o'clock,' I said as I gulped down my coffee and clicked on the payment button to confirm my flight booking. He rolled his eyes and asked with a sceptical look, 'And when are you coming back?'

'Next week…listen, please receive any letters that come for me. I've told the security guard too,' I said, fiddling with the coffee spoon.

I had met Vishal in a hotel on the first day I came to Mumbai in July 2011. Both of us had finished college and, like many others, we had come to Mumbai to become Mamma's best engineer betas. We belonged to that section of the Indian population which spent four years in engineering colleges measuring the figures of girls, studying about their virginity and discussing all possible types of bras; and were pushed into the hell of the IT industry. Here there were only sagging boobs, loose dicks and a completely frustrating life.

Smart people become friends when they know they have to follow a common path. We, too, followed the same rule and became friends and, later on, flatmates.

'Hey, are you going out? I need a print out of my ticket,' I said as I copied the ticket onto a pen drive. 'Okay.' He took it and left the room. 'Do you need anything else?' he shouted from the hall. 'No,' I said and he walked out, closing the door.

∽

'What the hell is this in my bag?' I muttered. As soon as Vishal got back, I asked him, 'What's this?'

'Condoms with extra dots,' he smiled very innocently, as if he was talking about them for the first time…a white lie. He knew about all the brands and flavours of condoms. After all, all of us had used them as birthday balloons in college as condoms were easier to get our hands on than balloons.

'Who the hell put this packet in my bag? I carry this to office and at times even girls reach into my bag for things.'

'How does it matter? This is for their use, after all! *Jaankari hi bachav hai*, don't you know?' As he talked, he took the packet, tore one, inflated it, and hit me with it.

'Stop it, Vishal, you're such a…' Once again, I checked everything—bags, cash and gifts for Anushka, Kavya and Navya. I was meeting them after a long time in Delhi.

Next day, I took a flight from the Chhatrapati Shivaji domestic airport and reached Delhi early in the morning at 7.15 a.m. Initially, I didn't want to go to Delhi but I couldn't say no to my mother who was dedicated to maintaining social ties. I was expected to be in Delhi to attend my elder cousin Navya's wedding.

∽

I took the metro from the airport to Connaught Place where Kavya was supposed to pick me up. 'Mom, do I have to attend this marriage ceremony alone? Why aren't you coming? Everybody is asking about you and I'm tired of answering these queries.' I ran my tongue over my parched lips. It wasn't too hot but was hot enough to make me thirsty.

Holding the cell phone in one hand and the trolley bag in another, I was standing at the CP metro station with no clue about which gate Kavya was going to emerge from. Kavya was my hipster cousin, three years younger than me, and we were the best of friends. I always saved her from Chachiji's questions when she was out with her hostel friends for night-outs. Often on these occasions we used to whisper to each other—*Aankhon se surma churana toh hamari aadat thi.*

Navya was known as 'Hitler didi' because of her dictatorial behaviour and she always kept an eye on us. However, tomorrow those eyes were going to be fixed somewhere else. Tomorrow was her mehendi—the day every girl dreams about, one that brings myriad colours into her life.

'You know your dad has gone out of station for some office work. Your Chachaji will be very upset if nobody from our family attends Navya's wedding. You shouldn't forget that you too have an elder sister—who will come to her marriage if we don't attend their weddings?' Mom gave me a lecture on my social responsibilities in answer to just one question of mine. Mothers will be mothers!

'Okay, but I don't like him. He has cheated us and taken all the money, land and savings of grandpa and even the gold coins that you got in your marriage and here I am, serving him! Is that not enough?' I shrugged, wanting to change the topic but mom had not taken my comments well.

'I have saved enough for you. Don't be greedy like others,' she replied diplomatically.

'Mom, it's not about what I have, it's about what my father earned for his entire life and left in grandpa's custody. I could have forgiven even that but cheating grandpa and taking his signatures on fake papers was the limit! I just can't accept that.' I realized I was shouting when I noticed that people were turning to stare at me as they passed by. 'I'll talk you later,' I told mom, feeling upset.

'By the way, I've called Kavya. She'll take care of you. And don't meddle in the affairs of others,' mom said compelled by her forgiving nature that was difficult to bear at times. To be truthful it is great, but to suffer and accept everything even when it is unfair is never fruitful.

'Where are you right now?' mom enquired.

'I'm waiting here at CP for Kavya and her friend to pick me up,' I answered.

'Okay, take care of yourself And give me a call once you reach home, I need to talk to Navya. I've sent some jewellery and bangles for her,' mom said. I walked towards the yellow line, looking at those pretty girls.

Irrespective of what time of the day it is, Delhi always has a fresh look about it and the credit for this goes to Delhi girls.

How do they manage to put on so much make-up? It's early morning and here they are, complete with mascara, lip gloss and eye liner, wearing the latest collection of fashionable, branded kurtis, I thought.

My eyes fell upon a group of pretty girls who were waiting for the metro. I realized that the glow on their faces and their confidence was what made Indian women so special. These qualities really set them apart and made a great case for Indian beauty being the best in the world.

Standing there I remembered those days with Pakhi in Delhi when I used to wait for her. Nothing had changed in the last two years...if anything had changed, it was me and my circumstances. Before I could suppress the sudden stab of pain, I saw Anushka in the distance wave at me and I broke into a smile. She looked like the sun that rose from behind the mountains—stunning, heart-warming and pretty.

'Hey,' she said in her musical voice, throwing her hair back.

'Hey,' I smiled

'Surprised? Kavya told me that you're coming, so I thought of giving you a surprise,' she smiled sweetly.

'Where is she?' I asked.

'She's on her way.'

I remember the first time I met Anushka. She was gorging wildly on a hot dog in a restaurant, and I had laughed at her loudly.

Though I am still made to pay for that but that is a fair price in exchange for a friend like her. Shiny long honey-coloured hair, rosy red luscious lips, a heart-shaped face and her luminous blue eyes had always held my attention. Her wide mouth and the adorable dimples on her cheeks, her naughty but charming expressions always won the hearts of others. Pronounced cheekbones, a stunning smile, long eyelashes—she was beautiful.

She was Kavya's best friend and if we were to go by mathematics, then—

When A is equal to B and B is equal to C, then A is equal to C, so I was C in this friendship between A and B for the past two years. Anushka became a very good friend of mine and she was my naughtiest friend. *Punjabi girls always rock*, she used to say to me as she was a Punjabi girl. We had spent a good deal of time roaming around in the lanes of Connaught Place in Delhi. At times, her caring nature confused me. Her respect for me and the way she supported me in difficult situations made me wonder if she loved me. Friendship had a very different meaning for her and that was, in fact, more pleasant and truer than love.

Therefore I say—*Punjabi hearts always rock...and Punjabi kudiyan always hot.*

She gave me a loving smile and her voice was loud enough to attract the attention of those passing by. 'By the way, how are you, Romeo?'

'I'm good. How are you?' I smiled in return.

'I'm as awesome and cheerful as the last time. God has given us a beautiful life so I just live by trying to meet his expectations and by being happy.' She glanced at her reflection in her cell phone screen. 'By the way, looking good,' I said. She blushed and put her phone in her bag without saying a word...then suddenly both of us laughed. 'Let's go,' she said. We both walked towards the escalators.

'Why do girls like always pink?' I asked, looking at her pink

Baggit handbag.

She laughed. 'You haven't changed even a bit in the last six months. There is no definition of likes and dislikes. Well...pink suits me so I like wearing pink,' she cooed, pinching my cheek.

'But you've gained a lot of weight for sure...' I blinked innocently.

'Live life king size,' she said inflating her cheeks like a balloon and placing both her hands on her waist. 'By the way I was nominated for Miss Delhi this year and I am sure they are a better judge of beauty and brains.'

'Are they still alive after going through the torture of meeting you?'

'I'll kill you,' she punched me on my shoulder. Girls are always assessed on three bases—curves, beauty and intelligence, and she was blessed with all three equally. Her dimpled cheeks were enough inflame even ice. She was very attractive and had a good sense of humour.

We both were standing in front of CDD at CP metro station. Her cell phone beeped and she received the call and said, like a true-blue Delhi-ite, 'Where are you? Come soon, kamini.'

Before Anushka disconnected the call, Kavya came from the back and jumped on her, shouting in excitement.

We were all meeting after years so this was expected.

'Let's go,' Kavya said.

Lost in Dreams and Hijacked by Girls

After roaming around in CP all day, we took the metro when it started getting dark.

'Why are you looking so shy?' Anushka laughed at me as I stood by the door.

'I'm not looking shy, just tired,' I replied croakily.

'Oye Multan ke sultan, you can have fun even in the metro,' Kavya patted me on my arm and said in her playful voice, nudging Anushka. People around us glared at me and that was enough to make me embarrassed.

'Why do you girls always pull my leg?' I sighed and closed my eyes and my college days flashed in front of my eyes. She had looked after me from the day I had told her about Pakhi. She was one of my few friends who knew our story.

'Hey! You can sit for a while if you're tired... I hope you know what will happen to you after reaching HRC,' Anushka said pointing towards a seat in the corner and both of them giggled.

'HRC, why?' I asked, surprised.

'We are going Hard Rock Café, Saket,' Kavya said and Anushka nodded. That had been their plan all along, I guessed correctly.

They were standing at the door and I was standing just next to them, leaning on the wall. All of a sudden a group of college students boarded the metro at Central Secretariat. It seemed like they had all bunked their classes and were headed for some fun. Some of them sat on the floor where two coaches of the metro were joined and others were standing at the door. That place made me remember the times when Pakhi used to sit there with her dance group, 'Hans Gang'. They were from Hansraj College and were quite famous across Delhi University.

She used to say, 'Metro seats are only for elders and senior citizens, this is the best place to sit for us.' She was crazy.

A tall girl in a plaid coat wearing cat-eye glasses looked at me while my mind was flooded with one sweet memory after the other, which haunted me on a regular basis now. It felt like I was with my college friends.

I remembered when my friends placed a big cake on the table just outside my hostel room. As my roommate had broadcasted an invitation message through the IP messenger throughout the hostel, all those devils were in front of my room within a minute. We believed that free cake gave us more calories, love and memories to remember forever. Birthday bumps, chilled water, cake, kicks on my ass (sandals, shoes and hands, they used almost everything on me) and I was still smiling because it was my birthday.

Those rude friends...merciless devils...now I miss them all. Hope I could see them once again. My life changed completely after college. While in college, we grumbled every day, looking forward to the time when it would get over and we would get a good job. Now that we had reached that stage, we longed to be with each other again.

Back-slapping friends, numerous cups of tea on sleepless nights, so many stories and very little studying, it went on till the end of the very last semester. We all used to sit together in the canteen, sharing four samosas and a bottle of cold drink amongst a group of eight or ten friends. Few chapattis on a single plate and many takers... I really want my college days back—the silly fights, canteen food, the exciting gossip...imitating lecturers, cursing them. Though we were loaded with assignments and projects, we had fun in our own way, which we miss now. In the evening, we all used to walk together...so much laughter, such happiness, no anger and no pride. Dinner was just an excuse to meet everyone at the same table. We enjoyed even in the classroom. Teased the professors, threw pieces of chalk at each other, ate chocolates, bunked classes, went for movies and never listened to anyone. Borrowing money was great fun, especially when it was used to spend on girls to gift them chocolates. There was very little money but a lot of love.

Then there were exams—the scary time. Last-minute notes, night-outs, pestering studious girls for their notes, watching latest movies before the exams and then finally waking up just an hour before the exam. Once the grades were out, we would sigh and promise ourselves that we'd do better next time and will score more for sure, but nothing changed in the next four years. During this beautiful journey, love blossomed in my heart and very dramatically, I met my love…my precious Pakhi. Life suddenly seemed brighter and more beautiful. Talking over the phone for the whole night, walking on the bridge alone but feeling as if the whole world was with you…I miss her the most.

Towards the end of this journey, placements came, and all of us got jobs. It was now the final week and we were in tears. Today, all of us have sufficient money to enjoy ourselves to eat fantastic food, to live a royal life but we don't have our friends with us—those who taught us how to walk in the journey of life. Today, we meet big personalities and attend meetings, but miss all those who taught us how to talk in an interview…

My eyes became wet and Kavya waved her hand in front of me and broke my reverie.

Eyes slightly squinted, scratching her nose, she asked, 'Hey, what happened, what are you thinking?'

I remained silent. Actually, I couldn't say anything as I was almost choking on emotions. 'Nothing,' I managed to reply.

'Not again, Anuj!' she said with mock anger as she realized that I was missing Pakhi.

'Nothing, I was just lost in my college days; I miss my friends a lot. How I wish I could meet them again!' I gave her a fake smile.

'You can try being friends with us, too. You can talk to us about everything, even about your sex life if you want…we won't stop you from doing so,' Anushka murmured flirtatiously.

'Shut up. He's my bro,' Kavya said, nudging her with her elbow.

'Let's go, our station has arrived,' cooed Anushka.

'The station never arrives. It is the train that reaches the station.' I laughed at her.

'So funny, let's go now,' she patted my back. Doors opened and we de-boarded the metro. 'Wait,' Anushka suddenly said.

'Now what happened?' Kavya stuffed her hands into her jeans pocket. Anushka's lips curled into a big bright smile, 'Mriga is also joining us. She's just reaching. She just pinged me on WhatsApp.'

A girl walked in from behind both of them and waved at us. I guessed that was Mriga and responded with a nod. I had not met her before but had heard about her from Kavya. Mriga put her finger on her lips and approached us silently. I nodded with a smile.

She sneaked up from behind and punched both of them on their backs and started laughing.

'Hello, babes.' They all hugged. Mriga was a sweet, innocent and decent girl. She didn't like partying much but went out for a few only with her best friends. She knew very well what she wanted from life. She was one of those girls who had never been in a relationship but had had numerous crushes starting from Ranbir Kapoor to her college seniors. Quite a few boys were attracted to her but she had a simple solution to stop them: 'I know we're good friends but I'm committed to someone else; how can I cheat on him?'

I couldn't stop laughing madly when I heard this crazy story. In the last month of her college, her classmate had proposed to her and she had replied, 'Deepak, I understand but my marriage has already been fixed for next month. I just finished distributing all the cards and don't have any left. Please do come with the others.'

After some time, I asked Kavya, 'Are we not going home? It's late.'

She came close to me and whispered, 'Don't get all melodramatic, let's just have fun.'

Few T-Shirts and Many Skirts

We reached Hard Rock Café. I was happy but somehow not comfortable as I was there with Anushka, Kavya and Mriga. However, that didn't matter for them. 'Be ready to rock, hero,' Anushka teased me, entering the gate. Mriga smiled and Kavya and I followed her gaze. HRC was in DLF Place, Saket—a vibrant, upscale shopping and leisure destination for well-heeled New Delhi citizens. It was quite an experience to visit that place. Spread over a large area with state-of-the-art facilities, HRC had a stage for live performances, and Hard Rock's signature retail Rock Shop. It had an irresistible menu consisting of classic American fare including burgers, sandwiches and salads, waiting to awaken your taste buds, while a *Meri Dilli* counter also represented local flavour, consisting of favourites like chicken kebabs and more. We all took our place just in front of the bar.

Unexpectedly, I was reminded of how when Pakhi and I were together, we were always on the look out for a decent place, less noisy and romantic... I smiled emotionally remembering those moments. We always preferred a place where we could talk and get to know each other than noisy, flashy places on initial dates.

These days couples go to famous, crowded places on first dates but they forget that even though they might be adventurous with food but that doesn't mean one has to experiment with food on the first few dates. It is more important to discover and know each other in surroundings where you are comfortable rather than knowing a new cuisine in a place where you are self-conscious.

After knowing each other well and sharing our feelings with each other we had a perfect and memorable date at a beautiful Indian restaurant where the decor, lighting, music and atmosphere were exactly as she liked. We enjoyed so many dates savouring each other's company. Moreover, every date added a new shade of colour to the abode of our love. We never showed our love in public places but were dedicated to each other. Our thoughts were always aligned as we believed that one rose was better than giving a bouquet of rare flowers, a gentle touch was better than public displays of affection. A smile would make each others' day and do a lot more than calling each other every moment to say we loved one another.

∽

'Where are you? Stuck on those chicks?' my hipster cousin Kavya asked, breaking my reverie.

'Nothing...,' I gave a smile and was brought back to the present. 'While you're here, don't forget to check out Hard Rock Café's world-famous memorabilia collection, including items representing contemporary stars, such as Buckcherry, 3 Doors Down and Black Eyed Peas, as well as pieces from musical legends like John Lennon, Elvis Presley, Tina Turner and Madonna,' Kavya finished in one go and then took a long breath.

'Is my cousin a "gone case" or are all girls like this? All you can think of is shopping and spending money and beautifying yourself...and you keep spending on the same things!' I asked Anushka while the other two craned their necks to listen.

'Because we have many things to show, you guys have only one and even that you can't really...' Mriga shot a six as I threw a bouncer. We had come to know each other enough in the last few hours for her to comfortably include herself in my crazy conversation with Kavya and Anushka. Shouting in a voice like a foghorn, Mriga said, 'I'm hungry. Need something to eat.' With a lopsided smile, Kavya nodded. I took the menu card and Anushka bit her nails.

Fragrances, music and dim light, the moment seemed so hazy and romantic, I just missed one person very badly...Pakhi.

Before I could start feeling sad once more, Mriga asked trying to make conversation, 'So how's it going in Mumbai?'

'It's pretty fine...Mumbai is a nice place to live in,' I turned to her and said.

'Yes, I've heard a lot about Mumbai's night life. So where do you go to enjoy your weekend?' she asked.

'When God made this life, he filled life with happiness and sadness and to balance that happiness for some people, he made IT industry,' I replied and they all laughed aloud.

'So...what's her name?' Mriga asked, taking a sip of water and wiped her lips with the back of her hand. Neither was it the right question nor the right time for it. Anushka and Kavya looked a little worried on hearing this as they knew how I felt when people asked about my past.

I knew what she was hinting at but pretended not to know anything. 'Who?' I asked.

'Where there is a night life, there is a girl,' said Anushka and Kavya together in a shrill voice to convert this question into a joke.

'It's not like that,' I answered simply.

Mriga looked at me, her prolonged eye contact making me uncomfortable for a while. She was not drunk but the depth of her eyes created some noise in my mind. I could see something in her eyes, but I ignored it.

In the month of December when Delhi was chilly and cold, all girls were looking super-hot in either skirts or hot-pants. They had enough spark to cause a fire in the bay.

Do all the girls come here to have fun? I asked myself. As usual, stupid strings of thoughts ran through my mind. Energized girls dominated the café as I could see only a few shirts and several skirts there.

✌

'Hey, I want one vodka shot, may I?' Anushka asked pointing to the bartender. It's very difficult to manage a girl when she is drunk. She can pull you into the worst situations, so I had one answer: 'I have the best answer for you and that is a big NO,' I cooed and pinched her softly on the cheeks.

'Please. Even I don't have an idea as to when I'd be coming here again. Just one, please...' she requested like an adamant child, almost pleading by the end of it.

'Yes, what's the big deal? Even as children we all had Dr Brandy, isn't it?' Kavya added fuel to the fire while Mriga was looking at us.

'Okay, then I'll tell aunty to give you Dr Brandy once we reach home, but as of now, no, you can't drink. We have to reach home before 11.00 p.m. else your mom will file a police complaint against me. Hope you understand. We'll try this next time for sure, okay?' I said in a serious tone to Anushka.

'If you won't allow me, then I'll tell my mom that you took advantage of us girls tonight,' she said gravely.

'Good try...I still can't allow you, sweetie,' I teased her.

'So mean you are.' But she remained seated, holding a glass and rolling the ice cubes in it.

The waiter served our food with a side of sour cream. Large potato shells fried golden brown and filled with Jack and Cheddar cheese, crisp seasoned bacon and green onions. I tried to keep her busy with the food and conversation so that she couldn't repeat that again.

'How's she?' Anushka twirled her potato skins with her fork. Mriga did the same and Kavya chewed the last bite.

'Who?' I asked, looking around. A bouncer, a burly black man with a goatee, caught my eye.

'That girl in ultra mini skirt with 34-24-32,' Anushka widened her eyes and slowly turned to the girl who was wearing a white T-shirt that had a few abstract drawings across the chest with these words at the bottom—'catch me if you can'. Her hair looked like someone had cut it with garden shears but she had perfect curves.

'Should I talk to her for you?' Mriga said, curling a tendril of hair around her finger and sipping a glass of pinacolada. I scoffed and growled at the same time.

'Okay. No problem,' she smirked and took a small sip of lemonade from Anushka's glass. The music became louder, and the air inside became hazier. All waiters came together and started dancing, standing on the small platform which separated the café in the bar from the other area. I had heard about the evening dance of HRC but it was a lot of fun to watch their sing-song movements. Mriga clapped down on the table in excitement. The smoke in the café was swirling around. Chilling time, ice cool glasses in hands, some with beer, some with soft drinks and only one with melting cubes of ice (mine).

'Happy?' Turning her eyes like juggler while snapping her fingers, Kavya asked me. She knew about the phase I had gone through in past few months.

'For what?' I questioned, finishing the last pieces of nachos from the plate.

'Are you not happy being here after a long time?' Anushka asked, expecting a reply in the affirmative.

'Hey! Thanks a lot for this.'

'Well, day after tomorrow I'm going back to Mumbai, you guys have fun.' I pinched her on her nose. I never wanted to leave them. After losing almost everything, I had only few things in my life—my BFFs (Best Friends Forever).

Kavya held my hand and assured me that everything would be fine.

'Hey brother, I'm always with you. I know I act stupid at times.

I created problems for you when mom caught me during college night-outs and she shouted at you but you didn't say anything. Not only you are a great lover, good son and a friend but you're also my genius brother. I'll miss you a lot.' I had never seen Kavya so emotional before.

'Hey! What happened? I know you're my naughty sister but why are you crying? Stop it,' I said.

'Can't you extend your stay?' Mriga asked, and both of them looked at me.

'I wish I could…Well, why don't you guys come to Mumbai?' I told them all.

'Yes, that would be great—at least I'd be happy. Every day mom forces me to cook from morning to evening. Moreover, my bloody neighbour always talks about my marriage…*beti badi ho gayi hai haath peele kar do*, bloody beep.'

We all laughed.

My wristwatch said it was 11.05 p.m. I had to reach before 11.00. 'Let's go guys,' I said, having a sip of water.

Anushka interrupted in between, 'Just one last shot of vodka.'

'What's that?' I asked her. Before I could confirm that she was having vodka, she had emptied the glass.

'When did you order this? Are you crazy?' I almost shouted at her.

'I'm sorry for that but I wanted to have just one peg,' she sounded completely drunk.

'What sorry, Anushka?' I shouted, clenching my fists.

'I have lost control over myself, please give me your hand and help me stand up,' she said. She swung to the other side. I stood up and held her, putting my hands on her shoulders and came out of the café. Everybody around was staring at us, especially at her and me, the way I held her and she hung on me. 'You know, you're my best friend. Only you can get me out of this,' she laughed. I held her hand; drunken Anushka was out of her senses.

A guy was staring at us and had been noticing us for quite some time. He came up to us and said, 'May I help you?'

'No. we're good. Thanks. I can manage.' I placed my jacket upon her shoulders and held her. He went away. Kavya was scared to go home. It was 11.15 p.m. and Chachiji had already called her twice and mom had called me just ten minutes back. This was going to be a big mess and I regretted coming here.

'We'll have to sleep on the road in this winter,' I answered in anger.

'I don't want to go, I don't want to go,' she sang.

'Now stop it, Anushka, control yourself,' Mriga held her waist and moved ahead. Kavya followed us. Getting these girls home safely was a herculean task for me. The streets were dark and deserted. The few street lights that were on were no better than years old oil lamps in the dense fog.

Delhi was never safe for women and as it was 11.20 p.m. in the night, I was scared. I was struggling to find an autorickshaw and after walking for almost a kilometre we found one on the other side of the road.

Anushka started laughing, 'Let's go now. Enough fun for the day.'

She gave a childish smile, very similar to the one I used to give my mother after stealing jam from the kitchen.

'Sorry, I just wanted us to have fun and to make this day memorable for us. Hope you won't forget...' she said, holding her ears in a gesture of asking for forgiveness.

She was not drunk. She had just pulled a prank on me.

'I'll kill you,' I tried to catch her. She laughed like the devil.

'How can I do this without your permission?' she said. I was angry but their craziness made me smile.

'We'll miss you. Don't make this moment sad. We enjoyed together and we'll meet soon,' Mriga said.

'Now we're getting late, let's go.' All four of us took an

autorickshaw and I preserved those moments in my heart.

Next day, I attended Navya's marriage ceremony and did everything as per my mom's expectations, and the day after, I was back to...

Candle in the Rain

$\mathcal{I}$ came to Mumbai after the few hours of happiness with Kavya, Anushka and Mriga and with dreams to make our own nest—a golden nest of love but before I could collect and weave twigs and grass together, a storm came one night and destroyed everything. I could neither cherish my dreams nor attempt to rebuild the nest. The past again won over present and it kept playing it over and over in my mind.

I used to listen to the voicemails I had saved on my laptop in a loop and would just start crying, looking at all those photographs she shared with me. Sometimes I tried to hate them to feel better but I couldn't. I shouted alone in the room, started hitting my forehead on walls but nothing happened except the floor became wet with drops of blood and then I slept hugging my wet pillows tightly. I used to wake up in the middle of the night and switch on my laptop to stare at her photographs or mails expecting that someday she'll send me a voicemail to give me a surprise, but I forgot that nobody was there to look at me, remember me, miss me. I had deleted all the romantic movies which I used to watch with her from my laptop. I had deleted all the songs…everything except that video which I had made for her. I just went through the longest voicemail, played it and closed my eyes and tried to imagine her in front of me, kissing me on my cheeks, holding my hands and whispering into my ears, 'I love you, I'll never leave you.' Nevertheless, when I confronted the reality, I closed my eyes again but this time to hide my tears.

My life had become a free show. People started worthless and rubbish discussions about me. I tried to sleep on time but I couldn't as there were no night calls. I used to check my phone so many times but never had any calls and messages. However, every time I washed my tears and sat somewhere in the corner of the room, waiting. Slowly, as time passed, even my tears dried up. Everything else had gone with her...my dreams, my happiness, my smile, my feelings, my future and a lot more. I had changed a lot. I was the guy who always had fun with my friends but now my friends had started asking me, 'What happened, are you okay?'

I just showed them my fake smile now. I had learnt to wear a fake smile but it was tough and painful. When my close friends tried to ask me about my situation, I just yelled at them. When my mom called me and asked me, 'What happened, are you crying?' I just had one simple answer, 'No, mom, I've caught a cold,' and then disconnected the phone, cried again and asked again myself, 'Is this love?'

∞

It was 10.30 p.m. when I stood up and came to the window. It was raining outside. I leaned back against the wall and sank to the floor, holding my knees together.

I looked at one of the old emails in my mailbox that she sent me after a fight we had. I went through each line multiple times. That mail said:

Hi Anuj,

Please read this mail with patience. I know we have had many fights in the last few days. I want to share a lot of things with you. Anuj, I know I'm the reason for all the fights but it is true that I love you a lot and want you to be happy.

Please remove the thought from your mind that I want to leave you. Why should I leave you?

I love you so much and you love me so much. A guy who takes care of everything in my life, why should I leave him?

Anuj, you're the one who wakes me up early in the morning, who puts me to sleep, makes me laugh and who makes me cry. I'm nothing without you, Anuj...please baccha, I really love you and will never leave you and I want your support. You pamper me like a small child as my dad used to; that's why sometimes I talk to you rudely but I really love you.

Hope after reading this, we'll share a tight hug...I'm waiting for your hug!

Yours,
Pakhi.

Tere gham ki silwaton mein kuch yun simta,
Ki aaine ne bhi thukra diya.
Jab koshish ki tujhe bhulane ki,
Teri yaadon ne phir se diwana bana diya.

I smiled without any reason. Messages, calls, late-night romantic conversations and kisses over the phone early in the morning—I missed all of it.

Tears were wetting my cheeks continuously and I was remembering those moments and felt strangely like a vacuum had developed in my stomach. Why couldn't I freeze those moments? Is it not possible to get those days back? What wrong have I done in my life that God has given me such pain? These questions kept floating in my mind.

I put my right hand outside the window and felt a few drops

of fall on it. I kept my palm open, felt the coldness of rainwater, and closed my eyes tightly. Outside, the earth was soaking in the sky's tears and under the roof, it was my heart.

'Hey, what are you doing here?' Vishal looked at me and asked entering the hall. He looked happy.

'Nothing,' I said, sniffing and hoping that he hadn't heard it.

'What are you doing here alone?' he asked me again.

'Nothing, it's raining. I love Mumbai just because of these rains.' I stood up and craned my neck outside the sliding window. He came by my side and looked at the dark sky. I couldn't stop myself and sniffed again.

'By the way, who was it over the phone? Was she my bhabhi?' I asked him to distract him as he was talking to someone a few minutes ago.

'No, not your bhabhi, but my bhaiya and bhabhi are coming to Mumbai next week. I'm feeling very sleepy, have to get up early morning. You also sleep. Good night.' He left the hall and went to his room.

I sat back again and stared at myself in the glass of the sliding window and some weird thoughts came to my mind. My friends used to talk about sex and porn movies. They used to go outside, enjoyed beer, whisky, and even had sex with girls. In the last month of college, Raghav and his friends had gone to the red light area. Raghav had spent a night with a call girl in a hotel. I had kept myself away from all those things because when I was leaving home, my mother had told me one thing—God has created us all in his image, bestowing us with qualities and abilities. It is up to you what you make of yourself and your life. I always followed what my family and friends expected of me, so why then was all this happening to me? I had never hurt anyone in my life, then why was I so alone?

Vishal came after ten minutes with a glass of juice and a grilled sandwich in his hands. 'Have this,' he said.

I was taken aback. I stood up and wiped my face. 'Hey,' I said.

He put the glass on the window sill and kept the sandwich on top of the glass and put his hand on my shoulder, 'Chal, kuch kha le.'

'I don't want to,' I said.

'Have something. Hold it.'

'Please, I don't want to eat anything,' I almost shouted at him. I didn't mean to shout but didn't know why I behaved like that. 'I'm sorry but I really I don't want to,' I said and looked at him with my wet eyes.

'It's okay. Well...I should not ask for a few precious minutes of yours, still...show some mercy.' He sat next to me and tried to make me laugh.

'Can't I get back my old days?' I asked.

Vishal was with me from the first day I had come to Mumbai. Him being my friend and then flatmate, I had shared everything there was to know about my life as he was so nice and kind. From waking me up in the morning to calling me for dinner in the evening, he had cared tirelessly for me. It's rare to find a gentle friend these days but I had, and I was incredibly lucky. 'It is raining even in Chandigarh,' he said. He had heard me but was trying to change the topic as he was aware of the truth that Pakhi won't come back in my life.

'Can't I get back my days?' I said again, a little louder this time.

'Anuj, this is not the end, you have everything one needs to live a good life. I know it is tough to forget the past but it is not impossible and it doesn't mean you should stop living your life. A girl comes and goes but you shouldn't change the way you live.'

'But...'

'No ifs and buts,' he said firmly, handing me the glass of juice. 'Come, let's go for a walk,' he said after I had finished the juice. We went downstairs, walked for a few minutes.

You make me laugh when I cry,
Without you, my smiles becomes wry.
You hold my hands when I look at you,
You tease me when I tease you.
You tease me but still I keep laughing,
But I've no fear because you keep watching.
I have done all wrong things with you,
But never walked a step ahead without consulting you.
There is no regret in life when I'm with you,
I am really lucky that I have a friend like you.

The City of Lord Ganesha

A long happy life can be lived just with those small smiles. Mumbai was still very new for me. Mumbai—the name I had heard in movies, newspapers and on news channels, especially during rains, but had never thought that I'll live with it, feel it and get to know it so closely. A city that never sleeps and is abuzz with a purpose and excitement. There are opportunities galore and it holds a promise to help you realize your dreams. The place is magical; you can become a millionaire even if you come here without a single penny in your pocket. It is a city that makes you feel secure even as you walk down its busy streets and the people around you help you even when they are in a hurry. Mumbai treats everyone equally—whether you are a CEO of a company or a modest hawker. A trip in one of the local trains in the morning is enough to make this fact evident as one sees some people wearing ties and suits, some stuck on office calls and some dreamy-eyed aspiring people—all of them travelling together and working towards fulfilling their dreams.

It is a place where everything is possible, where all your dreams come true, where you can talk to yourself, the place where you can feel those waves of life. Each moment leaves you with a lesson—to live, to know the reality of life—and gives you a purpose to live. I had been living in this city but still couldn't understand why I was there...the one I came to Mumbai for wasn't with me.

It was early morning in late August. The rain had reduced to a drizzle and I was waiting for my office bus. The coolest days of the monsoon season were over. Standing at the bus stop, I was listening to Jeeturaaj on Radio Mirchi. His Sanskrit shlokas were spreading the message of peace and prosperity while announcing that Ganesha had arrived to dwell in the hearts of Mumbaikars. Ganesha Utsav is a spectacular festival, celebrated in the honour of Lord Ganesha. The elephant-headed god is worshiped for ten days from Bhadrapada Shudha Chaturthi to the Ananta Chaturdashi. It's celebrated all over India, but the maximum grandeur is witnessed in this magical city Mumbai and across the state of Maharashtra.

One of my Maharashtrian friends told me the story behind this great festival. History indicates that the famed Maratha ruler Chhatrapati Shivaji Maharaj introduced Ganesh Chaturthi celebrations to the state to promote culture and nationalism and the great freedom fighter Lokmanya Tilak transformed it into an organized public event in 1893.

I wasn't a complete theist but always believed that if you walk on the right path, people help you truly and if you have belief, truth and commitment, they help you till the very end.

I had heard that Lord Ganesha fulfils the wishes of his devotees, thus, being selfish, I decided to visit a puja as my life seemed to be rolling downhill, hoping my prayers might bring my life on track.

∽

My cell phone rang. 'Get up and take a bath. We're going tonight to Lalbaugcha Raja,' Payal said quickly and excited over the phone. I was quite surprised as I had never seen her so excited except before having paani puri on Friday evenings.

Payal was one of those brilliant people who got back-to-back promotions, appreciation and success in her life. She was my senior but it never felt like that. Sometimes, keeping everything aside, I used to tease her that she was a demanding professional because of the way she treated management and others in the office. She was born and brought up in Mumbai and was a complete Mumbaikar. If

I had tasted all varieties of spicy and tasty foods of Maharashtra, it was just because of her. One thing that always made me notice her was her dressing sense. Of course, she worked in an IT company, where all young eyes are fixed on the computer screens but never miss a sharp cleavage or awesome legs.

Sad as it is, a girl never knows how many eyes walk with her when she walks, she doesn't know how many eyes measure her when she sits and how many eyes take snapshots of that moment when she looks at those eyes and makes their nights beautiful and peaceful.

'Hmm.' I rolled in my bed and slept again.

'What "hmmm" Anuj! Get up and get ready. It's 6.30 a.m.,' she said.

'It's only 6.30 a.m.,' I mumbled.

'So what? Get up, Anuj.'

'Why do we have to wake up so early in the morning? I-T S-U-C-K-S,' I threw my sheet to the other side of the bed but shrunk again into it.

'Just five more minutes,' I begged as I knew she wouldn't spare me and pleaded for just five minutes of mercy.

'Okay, but promise me you're coming to office and we're going for Ganpati darshan.'

'Ganpati bappa morya, I'll come and we'll go. Now let me sleep for ten minutes.' I didn't even realize when those ten minutes took a Ferrari ride and sped off in no time. I woke up with loud knocks on the door and clock said 8.30 a.m.

'Shit, I'm late. That bloody Bansal will screw me in the office today. Don't know how I'll catch my bus...' I ran to the door as someone had been knocking for long and I thought it was a dream. When I opened the door, my neighbour's daughter Charu was there.

'Should I come later?' she said, looking uncomfortable and as I had come out in just my jockeys and a towel over my shoulders.

'Shit...' I turned back in a hurry but it was too late; she had already seen me in this avatar. 'I'm fucked today.' I went to the room, wore my shorts and came back to the door. What the hell! I realized she was smiling at me and the reason was apparent.

'We have organized a Ganpati pooja at home today in the evening. Please come and stay for dinner also,' she invited me. I gave her a fake smile and closed the door.

I was already late for office. Therefore, I slept again after snoozing the alarm for twenty minutes.

My cell phone beeped again. Manohar Bansal calling.

I picked up the call while lying in bed.

'Where are you today?' he asked.

'Hey, good morning. My roommate isn't well, nobody was there, so I just went to the hospital, will reach office by eleven.' I was a good actor in my school days so acting was not a tough task for me, and that worked actually.

'Okay, no problem. Take care of him. You can take leave for today.'

'No, I'll come to office. I've called his relatives; they'll take care of him.'

'No problem,' he said and disconnected the call. I took a bath and reached office.

Payal laughed at me during lunch when I told her that Bansal called and I gave that excuse. That was alright but I couldn't swallow the bite in my mouth when she started laughing like hell and told me that Bansal had seen Vishal in the cafeteria in the morning and he knew that he was my roommate.

'What the eff?' I sputtered while she laughed.

∞

After all the IT tamasha and avoiding him till the evening, finally Payal, Vishal, Anushka and I left office. 'Count one more wish for today,' Payal pushed me, sitting in the office bus. Suddenly I remembered something. I gave her a smile and looked outside the window. The noise around us couldn't stop those thoughts which had started echoing in my mind a few minutes back when Payal had pushed my elbow.

> *Kuch log kisi mod par yun he mil jate hain,*
> *Bina naam, bina rishton ke apna sa kar jate hain,*
> *Apne sath dein na dein, kuch log dil me ghar kar jate hain.*

Timpanists were playing their drums full of energy. We saw pot-bellied Ganpati sitting on the chariot decorated with flowers and kumkum and decked-up women, men and children dancing behind it. The sky roared with the words '*Ganpati bappa morya…pudhchya varshi laukar ya!*' The drumbeats touched each cell of my body. My body shivered and for the first time I felt the magic of Ganpati and pleasure of this holy and sacred occasion. It had been happening for the last ten days. In the streets, slums, roads, newspapers, radio stations…at every nukkad, every corner of Mumbai, there was only one call…*devo ke dev Ganpati*. It seemed like all of Mumbai had come together in the protection of Lord Ganesha. Crossing many small and big processions on the way, we reached the Lalbaugcha Raja pandal. Vishal bought laddoo for prashad and marigold flowers to offer at the feet of Lord Ganesha. We offer marigold flowers to gods because it is special, as it can easily be divided into petals, showing the unity of diverse faiths and beliefs.

'People stand in this queue for two-three days to touch bappa's feet,' Anushka said, standing in a queue.

'Really?' Vishal asked and Payal nodded in approval. 'Yes, some stand even for ninety hours just to touch his feet.' I was happy that I found myself in this sacred queue.

There were many expectations in my mind but just one that I really wanted to be fulfiled, and I only wanted to share it with

Bappa. The pandal was so crowded that it seemed that the whole of Mumbai had come together. There were thousands of people but nobody had any complaints. There were smiles on their faces and wishes in their hearts—wishes to be happy, wishes for a prosperous life. I looked at Payal and Anushka. Both of them were wearing red bands on their foreheads and roaring *'Ganpati bappa morya'*. We moved ahead and my eyes got moist the first time I looked at this huge, magnanimous idol of Ganpati. It was forty feet tall and no one could imagine not being blessed at Lalbaugcha Raja.

The joy and fervour all around us made us feel happy, blessed and prosperous. There are two main queues in this pandal—the 'mukh darshan' queue that offered viewing from a distance of around ten metres away and was usually much faster, and the 'navas' queue for those wanted to make a vow or get a wish fulfiled (navas). The navas queue took devotees right up till Ganpati's feet. You could almost talk to the idol. It was common for the navas queue to stretch snake-like for over five kilometres. As I had heard, this queue guaranteed the fulfilment of whatever one wished for and I was there to share my pain with my Ganpati. Thus, I was standing in the navas queue with Anushka, Vishal and Payal. The hands of my wristwatch turned to 7.30 p.m., 11.30 p.m., 1.00 a.m., and 3.30 a.m.; finally at 5.00 a.m., I could see him in the form that I had heard so much about. I was quiet for a long time till I touched his feet, and devoted myself to him.

My belief in God as a myth was gone. A partial atheist was a complete devotee of Lord Ganesha now. I believed that only hard work matters; yes, it matters, but trust, beliefs, hopes and wishes give one a positive atmosphere to achieve goals, and fulfil dreams. When you believe in God then he's just next to you. Whatever you do, whatever you think and whatever you want, his eyes are always on you.

Spread love, you will get the same in return.

People smeared their foreheads with kumkum from Ganpati's

feet. Most of them also came to thank him for success, prosperity and gracing them with kids and life partners.

Many businesspersons wearing white kurtas offered golden coins at his feet. Even Salman Khan, the film star, came for a few minutes, creating a lot of commotion in the pandal.

We came back with several unfulfiled wishes in my heart. Lying in my bed, thinking about the moments I had actually lived after a long time brought a smile to my face and a ray of hope in my heart. I slept with my pillow that night.

IT Industry Nautanki

After devoting one whole night to Lord Ganesh, my days again started with irregular struggles of life. It was very difficult to forget those days I had spent with Pakhi. My life was just like a bar dancer who entertained everyone but nobody looked at her emotions, feelings and hardship. Is life just like that? I tried to find the answer to this question but couldn't. There was a time when I used to call one friend and many would appear in front of me but time had changed, nobody came to anyone without any reason. If they came, then there was smell of selfishness in their presence. You hardly find a true friend these days, you only read about Krishna-Sudama's friendship in books.

A true friend is someone who sticks by you when you are down and celebrates with you when you are up. It's someone you trust. It is someone who understands you, knows the real you and appreciates the person you are. When you help someone from your heart, he/she believes in you, he/she trusts you and then he/she searches for a true friend in you.

I missed my friends who were not with me. I had lost them because I had given more importance to love. My friendship with Vishal was different. We argued sometimes but we were good friends. When there is only one boat in the middle of the sea, you don't wait; you have to step into that boat. A new place and no known people made us CSC friends—Casual, Situational and Close.

Casual friends meet you for dinner, lunch and appreciate each other. So did we. I appreciated him when he couldn't talk to a girl in the office even after a few months of joining work and told him to consult a doctor, as his hormones weren't working properly. He also appreciated my patience when my manager shouted at me in the office. Then we would both abuse him as much as we could and laugh like hell.

Situational friends meet you at various points of time. Therefore, he was always there when I forgot to file tax, when I forgot to collect sodexo coupons from office and when I forgot to take medicines. Even I was always there. I was just behind him when he bought two cups of coffee—one for himself and the other for his office colleague Swati—and forgot to carry his wallet.

Close friends are those with whom you can discuss all your dreams, wishes and problems, with whom you can discuss all weird things and so did we. Vishal wasn't at all innocent, we discussed all the varieties, brands and sizes of bras—bandeau, bridal, adhesive, convertible, built-in, front-closure, demi, full support, minimizer, nursing, peephole, padded, push-up, softcup, strapless, sports, underwire, u-plunge and the water/silicone-cupped bra to make the boobs look big. That wasn't the end. We debated and concluded that the boob size 34C was the perfect size for a girl of average height.

∞

The lift door opened and I stepped out. Meera was standing there in the life lobby.

'Hey, good morning,' I wished her.

Meera darted across the lobby saying, 'Hey, good morning, how are you?' Her short blonde hair bouncing against her back, her sleeves fluttering, and her high heels clacking against the tiled floor. I synchronized my steps with her and said, 'I'm good. How are you?'

'I'm always good when I see you,' she laughed.

'I love the way you live your life, while being a software

engineer,' I teased her.

'That is because I love my work and if I am not wrong, even you stay here till late and work,' she said.

'Oh! That is not for the love for IT. I always wanted to be a singer or a guitarist but sadly, the Indian obsession "to become an engineer" overpowered those desires,' I simpered in a dry voice and explained what I wanted from my life. She started laughing, placing her hand on her rosy lips and curling a tendril of hair around her finger. Then she said, 'You sing? Oh please, don't tell me.'

'I'm not joking!'

She was still laughing. 'Enough...I have to go for a meeting, please stop it.'

Meera was my colleague, an American girl by her mannerisms and an Indian at heart. She had an innocent face and her teddy nose made her especially cute. She was born and brought up in Delhi. Her family had moved to Chicago when she had completed her fifth standard from DPS. From the last few months, Meera was working with our offshore team and we had become very good friends. Not only was she a good-natured girl but she was also ambitious, passionate and a smart resource for the organization. I always used to tease her when we all sat together during lunchtime at office by asking what she had for lunch to enable her to work hard till late at night.

I was sitting in the glass wall bay on the ninth floor of my office like every day. Very few months had passed but I had understood that no magical guru will come to help me here and only one thing could save me—I had to make my own name in this IT company cum political party.

In this industry, your boss says, 'You should concentrate on your work,' when you try to do other things and when you concentrate on your work, he says at the time of appraisal, 'You have worked only on one thing; increase your knowledge and skills in other areas too. You need to work on multi-tasking.'

There were many who were just running in the race—the race to get a few performance points, to get some appraisal mails and some perks with your salary. Nevertheless, I wasn't untouched by the reality and I was also one of those robots who worked hard from morning to evening, because I had not forgotten Charles Darwin's theory of the survival of the fittest.

∞

Another pop-up flashed on my computer screen. It was an appreciation mail from Manohar Bansal, assistant manager of the TISCO project, to Yash for the implementation of another tool. It was the fourth tool he had created in the last five months. None of these tools were used in the firm but they helped him in getting appraisals.

Fw: Multi Script Runner Implemented

From: Bansal, Manohar
Sent: 19 November 2012, 11.05
To: Gaur, Yash
Cc: Development_offshore

Great work Yash.
Team, I encourage you to make some tools like this.

Kind regards
Manohar Bansal

Please do not print this email unless it is necessary. Spread & *Encourage environmental awareness. AVOID PLASTICS!!! GROW TREES!!! SAVE NATURE!!!*

From: Gaur, Yash
Sent: 19 November 2011 10.51
To: Development_Offshore
Cc: Katiyar, Seema; Bansal, Rohini

Subject: Multi Script Runner Implemented

Hi Manohar/Seema,
A tool has been created that can help in software testing.

Problem:
Running multiple jobs repeatedly is quite a big ache for a tester when it needs to be executed numerous times, also keeping the track of logs of whether the job has been successfully executed or not is a tedious job to be done?

Solution:
So here is a solution! Multi Script Runner is a tool that converts all the scripts into a single script.

Benefits:
• Tester need not remember the name of jobs and escapes from typing it repeatedly.
• It saves time and increases revenue.
• We all should use this tool to get beneficial results.

Thanks to Sonal, who helped in creating the code. We both can create more tools together in future; she has enough knowledge developing such tools.

Thanks to Payal for her input.

Thanks to Seema for the idea that motivated
us in the creation of a handy and effort-
saving tool.

Warm regards,
Yash Gaur

I smiled looking at the mail and before I could read it completely, Payal approached me in anger. She pulled up a chair and sat right next to me. 'What the hell!' she blurted out. She seemed angry and tense. I looked at her, gave time to her to release her anger and asked, 'what happened?'

'Did you see the mail?' she asked, coming close to my PC and snatching my mouse.

'Yes, that mail about multi script runner. Congrats,' I said, as I knew she had been working on that for the last few weeks. Then I looked at her face—she looked very disappointed. 'So, what happened?' I asked.

'I have been staying till late in the office since last week. I gave him the code, layout, all input parameters and...see,' she pointed to the mail that was open on the computer. I didn't say anything because I had seen that she stayed at office and worked hard till late in the night.

'Clam down. Everybody is here,' I said, looking around.

'That B-I-T-C-H Sonal, all day she talks to her boyfriend, leaves office at sharp 6 p.m. and see? "Thanks to Sonal, who helped in creating the code..."' She put her hand on her forehead in frustration.

'It's okay, Payal, it happens and this is not new, right,' I opened the water bottle and passed it to her.

'But this time I really worked hard,' she pleaded.

'Then talk to Manohar and tell him everything. Come, let's go to the breakout area.' I stepped out and she followed. This wasn't new in our office. This IT nautanki was going on from the day I joined.

Everybody was running in the race to impress, to get promoted, to get good ratings and didn't think once before hurting others and cheating them.

'Did you talk to Seema?' I asked as I took two cups of coffee from the coffee vending machine.

In a helpless voice, she took the coffee mug and sipped once, 'No, and I have already had a discussion with her regarding the implementation but she didn't approve my idea and that dickhead has gone and done the same thing.'

'Anger isn't the solution of anything, just relax. Talk to Seema and tell her that your contribution was much bigger and that you worked very hard on this.'

Payal wasn't in a mood to listen. 'Let's go. Sagar has some plans so have to leave just after office,' she said. Sagar was her boyfriend and worked with another IT company. We both left the cafeteria and she left the office after few minutes.

∞

The sun had gone behind the hills and now it was dusk outside the office. Slowly the hands of the clock reached 8.30 p.m. but I had to fix some code issues.

There were a few more unlucky creatures sitting in the next aisle, wasting their life fixing codes in the IT industry rather than fixing codes in their life.

Since joining the IT industry, I had been trying to find at least one person who seemed happy with their job, but it had proved to be an impossible task.

Those who were unmarried still had some peace; at least they weren't worried about their life partner's extramarital affairs. The reasons were simple. Males who were working the whole day at office didn't have any interest I taking off their wives' bras and there were high chances that, as a consequence, other ready creatures were getting the opportunity of opening them. If they couldn't make their night pleasurable then their wives started looking for other toys and boys.

Good sex ensures a good and healthy life and bad sex certifies that you're an IT engineer. Moreover, the same applies to women in the industry and their husbands, too.

Early in the morning, I changed the status of the office communicator that said: 'Those who wake up when the world sleeps, the world salutes them when they sleep'. Before I could change it to: 'We wake up when US clients sleep; we work till the day we breathe', someone put a hand on my shoulder. I turned suddenly.

'Oh, you're still here. Why haven't you gone home?' Meera said, surprised. 'Even your best friend, Payal, has left, so what're you doing here?' she said teasingly.

I rolled my eyes. She asked too many questions.

'Yes, almost finished. Just wrapping up,' I said, rubbing my eyes. She smiled as usual and that was enough to make me happy, at least for some time. 'One day I'll die sitting in this chair, doing this work. When will I live my life? Who will remember that I created a defect-free code and executed it without any failure. Who will remember that I got the extra bonus? At the end of the day we all have to go there...people will remember you, not your money...' When I abruptly stood up to stretch my body after sitting in the chair continuously for five hours, these thought came to my mind.

Then I suddenly remembered what Vishal had told me. It was funny but true—Americans are hardworking because they don't use their dick where they actually have to use their minds, not like us where people use their dicks rather than using their minds. Even their government, which is one of the best in the world for their people, is not like ours where our prime minister opens his mouth on a few occasions annually. I laughed silently, and ended up coughing.

'What happened?' she asked. Her red cheeks, brown eyes, cute nose...I thought about the incident at lunch when she had slapped me on my face in a joke and I had acted as if I was badly hurt and the security guards had came to the bay.

This time I laughed aloud. 'Nothing. You should be in jail,' I sat back in my chair. She laughed, putting her hands on her mouth...a devil's laugh, carefree and hearty. Voices echoed in the whole bay and she punched her fist a couple of times on the desk as a judge would do in the court. Still laughing, she continued, 'But you're crazy. The way you acted!' We just laughed. If someone else heard it, they couldn't guess whether it was a laugh or a shriek.

'Hey stop...' I held her hand. Someone punched an access card at the entry door of the bay as we heard a small beep. I raised my neck to see. The security person had come into the bay. I looked at her.

'What happened?' Meera asked, squeezing my hand and raising her neck to look at the security guard in a black coat. We both remained seated as we were.

'Is everything fine?' the security guard asked. I laughed in my head.

'Yes,' she replied in a very serious tone. He took a round till the end of the bay and left from the other exit.

'Now enough, let's go out,' Meera tapped my shoulder.

'Is there something special today?' I asked.

'Nothing special but I want to go out and you're coming with me,' she said confidently, but she was looking prettier than she normally did, and I guessed there was some reason for her to stay late at the office.

'Nooo...' I replied as I wasn't in a mood to go out because a few minutes back I had been going through three-year-old messages from Pakhi on my cell phone and I was missing her badly.

'Just for a cup of coffee outside at Barista or somewhere you want? Juhu beach?' Meera pleaded but she knew I won't say no as beaches were my favourite places because they helped me find peace in their waves.

'Have you ever tried a career of manipulating people?' I said to her.

'No. Why?' she asked mischievously, knowing she had won the argument.

'You're really good at that. Let's go.' I packed my bag and stood up.

She laughed, 'Funny...'

'Okay. Drop me to my place. Let's have coffee there and then you're free to go. Simple, isn't it?' she said very confidently.

She lives alone. Should I go there at this time? I thought.

'Sure, I can drop you, but is it really important to stay there?' I questioned.

'I'm not asking you to spend the whole night with me, okay,' she laughed, raising her eyebrows, and threw her stole around her neck.

'Okay, let's go,' I smiled and we both left the office. We hired an autorickshaw.

∞

'So...how do you manage everything? You wake up early in the morning, write, get ready to come to office, work till late at night, go back and then write again, and then plan for the next day! On weekends you work with NGOs for children, and in between you visit colleges and corporates to give speeches as well. That doesn't sound manageable!' she asked me.

Nobody knew why I was doing all this. I just wanted to be busy every second of my day. I never wanted to remember my past because those memories made me cry.

I smiled and said, 'When I left my home for studies, my dad told me only one thing—one day we all have to sleep, so let's work hard till the day we breathe. You've got twenty-four hours and I've got my own watch.'

She smiled too. We got off near Hotel Leela and walked to her apartment. After walking for five minutes, we reached her place. She unlocked the door.

'Come in,' she said and threw her handbag on the sofa.

'Thanks,' I said and closed the door. Her place was beautiful and very different from other houses I had seen. It was decorated with stickers, cartoons, wind chimes and chandeliers. It looked like an old American house.

'My sexy lady forgot her papers. Now she'll shout at me.' She took a few papers and put them into the cupboard.

'Who?' I asked.

'My mom,' she grinned.

I sat on a chair near a table which was piled up with papers and files and a fruit basket. I could smell coffee in every corner of her house. 'You are crazy about coffee, isn't it?' I asked, standing and looking at the portrait of, I guessed, her mom and dad. She looked at me, her lips pressed together and eyes squinting, and asked, 'Why?' She offered me a water bottle and went into the kitchen. 'This is your mom and dad's portrait, right?' I asked.

She peeped from the kitchen, 'Oh, yes my mom and dad's twenty-fifth marriage anniversary, Back Forty West, New York City.'

'Sugar?' she asked.

'Not too much.'

'By the way, I can help you,' she said, holding a kettle in her hand. She came to the hall put the kettle on the table. She filled two spoons of coffee powder in cups and one in her mouth. Then she poured water in the cups.

'I'm not suffering from any disease. Help for what?' I asked placing my hand on the table.

'Denial is the first sign that you don't accept it,' she smiled and took a sip of coffee. 'Perfect.'

'Why don't you move on, Anuj? Have you ever looked at yourself?' She gave me a cup of coffee and sat on the chair. 'You have many reasons to be happy. You're talented, you're hard working and you have a cute smile. Yes, you have a cute smile.' Wiping her mouth, she repeated it to make me smile.

'There are many things in life that we can't change. There are a few people in life whom we can't forget. It's tough to move on,' I said, putting the cup down on the table.

'But it's not impossible, Anuj,' she said, took a sip and continued, 'What life do you have? Which movie did you watch last? Do you even remember? Which restaurant have you gone to in the last six months? Moreover, keep your wallet. You forgot it at your desk in the office,' she laughed, handing me my wallet. 'Do I still need to show you more proof?'

'Oh shit, how did I forget my wallet? I checked my other stuff as well,' I said, taking it from her.

'You'll go home, will put your shoes in the rack, clothes on the hangers and bag on the table. You'll prepare for tomorrow. You'll have dinner, watch TV to keep yourself busy and in the end, you will fall asleep. Just work, with no time for yourself. Am I right?'

I kept silent for a minute and thought about whatever she had said. She had said nothing wrong.

'I love to work,' I said.

'You love your work and that is great but you work because you don't want to remember those moments you spent with her; you work because you don't want to get time to think about her but till when are you going to do that? Come out from your shell,' she raised her voice.

'Let me find her once,' I said as that emptiness returned to my heart.

'And you know what, you're a complete package for romance. You can try even on me! If you can impress me, you can take advantage of me. I'm a rich girl,' she smiled and then blinked her eyes. A smile tells the truth and a smile with blinks says many things. I laughed.

'Advantage?' I laughed again. 'This is not a game for me to take advantage. Yes, you are a rich girl but I can't lose my friend who is priceless.' I pinched her on her nose. She looked at me like a small girl looking at her father. We both knew each other, believed strongly in each other.

'I can help you,' she said again.

'Help in what sense?'

'Every day, you have to come here after office. Have one cup of coffee with me and listen to whatever I say. And we will not talk about work.'

'That's interesting, but I can't promise anything. I'll think about it,' I said and stood up.

'It's not a big thing, just a coffee...and don't worry, I won't allow you take advantage of me,' she stood up too.

'It's late. See you on Monday at the office.' I shoved my wallet in the back pocket.

'I made you happy and smile, didn't I? Now you owe me a chocolate,' she smiled and came downstairs with me.

'Thanks for this time,' I smiled back.

'My pleasure, and you owe me a chocolate. Don't forget,' she waved as I walked to the other side of the road and caught an autorickshaw home.

When Life Seemed Over

While on my way home, I kept thinking about what Meera had said.

You need someone who can understand you when you are alone. You need someone to listen to you and tell you what the right path is when you are doubtful and helpless in life. I rang the doorbell.

Vishal opened the door. 'Hey, so late today?'

'Hmm, was busy at work,' I said and came to my room. I took a bath and sat in the hall, doing something with my laptop on the sofa.

'Hey, what happened? Why are you sitting here? Is everything okay?' Vishal asked.

'Yes, all fine. I have to finish some work so I'll sleep after some time.'

He went to his room and again, I started thinking about all the bad things about me, all the humiliation that I had suffered, all those days when people used to say, 'He is mad and insane. He's a duffer. He can't be my friend.' I started thinking and everything blacked out within seconds. I started feeling unwell. I was lying in my bed and thought staring at the fan: *What is my life? Neither am I happy nor am I doing anything that gives me happiness. Is it only about money?*

My mind argued at the next moment: *Yes, just money, money doesn't matter but when you don't have it matters a lot for survival, so work and earn.*

Then why do people finish themselves?' I looked again at the fan. What if I hang myself? Even if I lived, what would I do—just mental disturbance to my family and others? They have done everything for me and I don't even pick up their calls. I felt deeply annoyed. Those couple of medicines of fever and cold on Vishal's table came to my mind. *What will happen if I have all of those?*

I came to the room, switched on the light silently. Everything happened in a very positive way. I took all the eighteen to twenty tablets wrapped in a paper. Wrong things don't take much time to be executed.

I felt so comfortable doing this. And the motivation behind this was pain—the pain in my heart, my soul, my mind that tortured and made life too awful to bear.

Everything happened in a hurry but suddenly something came to my mind—Why didn't mom call me today?

'Fuck…what the hell am I doing?' I threw the pills across the room.

Vishal woke up and looked horrified. 'What happened?!' he screamed. Before I could say anything, I ran to the washbasin and vomited whatever I had eaten. Vishal ran towards the basin and he held me.

'I'm fine. You sleep,' I said.

He held my shoulder. 'Shut up. Come here and sit.' He sat with me on the sofa in the hall.

'What were you doing with these medicines?' he asked. I didn't speak. I felt like my head was burning and the rest of my body was getting cold.

'Tell me!' he shouted at me.

'Don't worry, I won't die,' I smiled with my dry lips. 'I need some water.'

He brought me a glass of water. 'I told you not to eat curd at night. Should we go to the doctor?'

'I am okay, you go and sleep. I'm fine. I think I just ate

something spicy and oily.'

'Are you sure?' He looked worried.

'I am fine,' I replied, took some water and went to bed after cleaning up.

'Okay, come and sleep.' He switched off the lights and kept dabbing my forehead with wet cotton. After some time, he fell asleep next to me on the bed.

I was uncomfortable and was not able to sleep. I felt like I wanted some fresh air. It seemed like everything was shrinking towards me. I stood up silently and ran to vomit again. I was scared. I tried to control myself and fell on the floor. I tried to stand up but felt too weak to get up. I couldn't even move my body to the sofa. Tears started flooding my eyes as I tried very hard to speak... I opened my mouth but no words came out.

Someone help me, please, someone come...please—I was shouting within but couldn't speak. Nobody was there. I crawled slowly and collapsed anyhow on the couch.

When I opened my eyes, it was 4.20 a.m. and I was being rushed to the emergency ward of the hospital.

∽

'Low blood pressure, nothing else, you're fine,' the doctor flashed a small torch on my retina. He smiled, holding a pen between his fingers. 'We just need to do some tests and you can go home in the evening.' He looked at me, holding the stethoscope in his hand. The doctor was talking to my neighbour uncle and Vishal.

'Did you call my parents?' I asked Vishal.

'No, should I?'

'No, please don't. I'm all well. They'll just get worried for no reason.'

'So, how are you now? The doctor said you are perfect. We can go in the evening,' he said.

The doctor came to my bed and asked, 'Do you have your

previous reports?' I took some time to answer because that question made me uncomfortable.

Why does he want my previous reports? I thought. 'Yes. I have them, doctor.'

'Okay, great, I just want to see those reports.'

The needle pricked my upper hand and I was looking at every drop of glucose dripping into my body...tip...tip...tip...and thinking, *Who knows my pain? Who knows my feelings? Who knows what I want? Who knows who I miss so much?*

Do those reports clarify those things? Never.

These were the unanswered questions that hurt my emotions and feelings deeply.

'The only thing you have to take care of is your health. Your blood pressure was 55/100 when you came here,' the doctor advised.

'Okay, doctor,' I nodded and tried to sit up with the support of the back of the bed.

The drab grey colour of the hospital walls never failed to throw a bucket of cold water over my spirits. That all-too-familiar smell that hospitals have—was it from some kind of medicine or was it from all that bleach?—floats around in the air like a constant presence, never wanting to go away and leaving me alone. I was starting to think that if I was stuck in this room for any longer, not only would I lose my sense of smell; I might start losing my sense of humour as well. As I sat here motionless in the hospital room, the scents of unidentifiable foods and medical substances invaded my nose. There was a dead silence, even as nurses and doctors conversed quite noisily outside my room. My eyes were fixed on a figure in the hospital ward.

Early next morning, Payal and Meera reached the hospital. They were scared and tensed and I could see those wet eyes and lines of worry on their faces. 'What happened to you?' Meera came and sat near my head on the bed.

'Nothing, I was getting bored at home,' I smiled.

'Shut up. How are you now?' She placed her hand on my forehead.

'I'm good; just need your black coffee.' I held her hand in mine.

'Sure.' She ran her hand through my hair. 'Just be well.' Women are a gift from God. They take your pain away and make you feel special every moment that they're near you. I felt something like that for a while but that was all in the past now.

After looking at my previous reports, the doctor discharged me in the evening. 'You need to take care of yourself and not think too much; life is so beautiful.' These words were the last words the doctor said to me when I took support of Payal and Vishal and sat in the cab.

Moreover, Meera was sitting in the front seat and wiping her eyes. Emotions don't depend on religion, colour or caste. Meera was the best example of that. Being American, her heart was still Hindustani.

As the cab dropped me off near my house, I saw the person who ran the tea stall on my lane looking at me. I wasn't sure who he was but people used to call him Rahim Chacha. Though I had never tried to talk to him, he continued staring for a while before looking away and continuing with his work.

Nine Jewels of Truth

These people stuffed fruits and their stupid lectures in my stomach for a fortnight and made sure that I was healed properly.

Everything changes with time but few things go on forever, like the love of a mother for her child and getting up early in the morning. Therefore, that day, after rolling for fifteen minutes in my bed, I woke up and brushed my teeth under the shower to save time. A minute is very important when a cat is behind a rat or a lion is behind a deer and a boss is behind an IT engineer. Therefore, it was better to skip breakfast rather than being late for office.

After all, I was going to work after a fortnight.

Nevertheless, one thing had been bothering me for the last few weeks. There was something about that old man who ran the tea stall just in front of the bus stop near my house. I wanted to know more about him because of the way he always looked at me—like a silent, non-interfering observer.

'Does he know me? But how?' was the question that I wanted to know the answer to. I reached my bus stop ten minutes earlier just to listen to him talk to others. Every day I used to look at him but ignored him like everybody else but I had already decided last night that I'd talk to him today.

He was about fifty years old if I was to go by his hands, the wrinkles on his cheeks and forehead and the crow's feet near his eyes. His salt and pepper hair and the handle-bar moustache always attracted my attention.

My Nanu once told me that those with handle-bar moustaches have many secrets and magic up their sleeves as he always told me magical and miraculous stories. That old man had some black marks on his hands and they were an indication of how hardworking he was and his eyes showed how experienced he was. I used to see him every day in front of the bus stop with his utensils and few spoons of extra sugar that he used to put in the kettle at last…That was weird…why extra? Yes, why extra, I wanted to know. He was quite famous in the neighbourhood just because of his belief in something extra or an extra spoon of sweetness.

'Stupid old man.' I ignored him as it was already too late and then I heard something that day: 'As your one percent extra effort makes you a leader when nothing remains, my one spoon of extra sugar makes my tea best and that makes your day.' The moment he stopped talking, I turned back.

He laughed cheerfully and looked happy, showing his white teeth. He smiled proudly raising his head to the sky, as if he was a great leader and ignored me this time

'What the fuck is that?' I said, feeling a little offended.

His love, dedication and happiness for his work had me captivated.

Everyone who had money and success in their lives were searching for happiness and rarely could find it and that old man didn't have enough money but was spreading happiness all around. He looked at me and smiled.

Does he know me? Why did he smile? Is he mad? No. He wasn't mad. I was reminded of a conversation he was having just a moment ago with another man who looked a corporate person as he was wearing a coat and a tie. 'But why was he talking to him?' These questions arose in my mind suddenly and burst like rainy bubbles. The bus turned right just before the stop. People standing with me moved a few steps ahead and I boarded the bus with them. I stared at him from the bus window and respected him by passing a smile too...

❦

His words had logic, motivated me and gave me many much food for thought.

Next day I reached the bus stop sooner just to listen to him. It seemed insane and this was very unusual for me but I was willing to change because his words gave me peace However, I was still not too sure about talking to him.

It was just like another day that I was standing there at the bus stop. He smiled at me and waved. It was weird but he called me to his tea stall. Initially I was feeling awkward but I thought that there was no reason to be afraid.

'I might as well go talk to him or he'll disturb me every day. At least I can listen to him once,' I thought. Mondays are the worst days for college classes and offices, so I thought spending time there would make the first day of the week better.

'Yes?' I looked at him and asked.

'You didn't come last Friday,' he asked.

'Oh, Friday was a holiday,' I replied, standing in front of his tea stall.

'Okay, so what did you do on Friday?' he asked me very eagerly. He placed his kettle on the stove and poured some water in it.

'Nothing as such, just rested,' I answered, passing him the matchbox. He wanted to know about the time I saw him from the cab, I guessed.

'Then you should do something,' he smiled and lit the stove.

'Yes,' I smiled. My bus turned the corner at the same time.

'Hey, see you tomorrow,' I walked with fast steps to catch my bus. He waved goodbye.

Days started changing and I started missing my bus to spend time with him. Day by day, that became a part of my life. Every day I used to have a cup of tea and we talked. He never charged for his special tea, so for me it was a win-win situation.

One day I asked him, 'Why don't you take money from me? That's against the business. If you'll do this with everyone then what will you earn?'

He started laughing and replied gracefully, 'If you want to give me money for this cup of tea then smile for me. It is priceless and I earn much more from your smiles. To answer your second question—not everything is saleable in this world. Sometimes, relationships are more important. By the way, I'm a good businessman, one day I'll tell you what I've got.'

Was he a preacher? Did God send him to guide me? If not, then who was he? Whoever he was, he knew a lot about life. Being a very normal person, he had a rich heart, beautiful thoughts and a happy life. I started meeting him on one pretext or the other and even on holidays.

✺

The last time he told me something was when he found me unhappy. He said, 'Sometimes I feel very bad when I look at those people who have money but no happiness. I feel bad when I see people who are fighting for success in office, in business and everywhere where they get more. Actually, they are not wrong; they've just understood life wrongly. They think life is a race and if they run, they will win the race. Nevertheless, life is not all about winning the race. Then what is the reason, why are we running? Though I'm not some guru but if I can help even a single person see the reality, I will think that I've done something meaningful in my life. Life will never come back, then why regret anything? Who knows what will happen tomorrow? If you want to fall in love, don't wait. If you want to be a symbol for society, for your country, for the world, then wake up, don't be lazy. If you want to say something, then don't let your tongue stop you. We all have dreams; we all have friends, family and love. They all love you so much. They all want to see you happy. They all want to see you as a successful person but with a smile, and that is important.

Working 24x7 in an office is not required to be happy but happiness in your heart gives you real success and makes you a successful person. Many times we hurt people and get success but winning hearts is actually a big thing in life; so just love those who love you and make them smile.

Something that was so simple yet so profound, which had remained untold and hidden, was told to me.

My ears longed to hear him every day. I started talking to him and he welcomed my stupid questions.

'Are you from a family of preachers?'

'I'll tell you once winter is here.'

'How is winter related to that?'

'Let's wait for winter and I've many things for you.' He treated me as my grandpa did when I was a child.

'This is just becoming filmy and dramatic. Please tell me what you wanted to earlier,' I asked him but he ignored me with a smile, saying that he will tell me for sure someday.

✍

While waiting for winters, I learnt many things from him—something new every day.

On one weekend, he opened up the treasure of his thoughts, which I accepted as the 'Nine Jewels of Truth'.

First thing he told me was—when the sky cries, birds start singing, then how can you expect others to not laugh when you cry? This is the 'rule of nature'.

Initiation is always important; doesn't matter how small it is. Sometimes your efforts don't give you success; they just give you patience and more courage to work hard for the next task. Problems and hurdles are more responsible for your success than comfort and pleasure. Holding a finger is not enough to learn how to walk, that makes you weak. To be the master of the world, you have to walk alone—'to drink in the healthy juice of loneliness and hard work.'

If you have lost something, you have also achieved something. Success doesn't depend on your genes, it actually depends on how you take the best from the worst and how you represent the worst as the best—'the beauty of perfection.'

Perfection in work and perfection in love, both are completely different in life. A loser can be a winner in love, a winner can be a loser in love, and the one who balances both is the real winner of the world—'the happiest creature of God.'

Don't wait to appreciate others and don't stop to correct someone. When you appreciate, you motivate yourself and when you correct someone, you wash out dust from the window from where you can look at your goals too—'the world is a mirror.'

If you close your eyes, obviously, you will see darkness even in the light, but if you have patience and open your eyes, for sure, you can find a spark even in the dark that is enough to win the battle—'the battle of love and life.'

Don't rate your perfection too soon, sometimes the last card of your hard work decides the winner—'the magic of patience.'

Don't flow with the rain of disorientation when you have the capability to sail your boat alone. Success is not all about snatching things and getting them. It never comes directly. You are the one who trusts you the most because you know yourself better than others do. You face, you learn, you experience, and as a reward, you get success. So never run for success because it's nowhere. Just listen to your soul's advice and follow your heart about which path you have to walk on. So stay committed, be loyal and be happy with yourself. Success or failure is not the end; you still have to win hearts—'that is real success.'

The magical fact—Save money at every happy moment that

comes in your life. Then see, one day you would be the richest person in life and have money too!

Things remain perfect only in movies and not in real life and the same happened with me. He was nowhere in my life but he had touched the threads of my heart and changed my life in the last one month. I started thinking good things about life, about people.

You never know when you meet amazing people and I met him. You can learn from a small kid or from an old man, no matter how old you are.

Always be a teacher and a learner for your entire life.

You'll get love and you'll spread love for the rest of your life.

Just like the extra spoon of sugar in his tea, he told me Krishna's story—When Krishna was a small child, his mother sent him to the gurukul for his education. Krishna said, 'Mother, I don't want to go. I'm happy at home and you're my best teacher because life gives so much and makes people cry.' His mother smiled and said, 'My son, if you'll stay here, you'll be my best student and my great son but when you'll go there you'll be the master of the world.'

Life Made Me a Bad Deal

When you're alone you search for a good friend in every face. When life was taking wrong turns, Kalki supported me and helped me as much she could.

Kalki was working with her own newspaper in Mumbai. I met Kalki when I had been begging for help while looking for Pakhi in Mumbai. As she was running a newspaper, she had contacts in online and print media. In fact, since I had friends like Anushka, Payal, Meera, and now Kalki, people had started teasing me by saying that I was like Krishna surrounded by his gopiyaan.

I accepted her in my life thinking of her as the Kalki avatar that is supposed to be the most powerful avatar of Lord Vishnu because it will signify the cleansing of the world from all its sorrows. Kalki's parents had passed away when she was just five. Her grandmother had taken care of her and had made her a successful girl. The way she had lived her life by facing problems and crossing hurdles and what she had achieved impressed me. I always felt good while talking to her because my life was similar to hers; the only difference being that her parents had left and in my case, my love.

We became good friends and I received a message one day from her—Hey, are you coming in the evening? I'll reach home by 7.00 p.m. Message me if you are coming. I presumed she wanted to meet me because she had more information to share about the search for Pakhi.

I wasn't feeling well since morning. I left office early and messaged her that I would reach by 7.30. Luckily, I reached earlier than that and went to a mall near her place. I messaged her—I'm here at the bookstore in the mall. She called me in a hurry saying that would reach there in a few minutes. I was turning pages of books at the store and then someone said, 'Hey.'

'Hey, Kalki, how are you?' I turned and looked at her.

~

'I'm good. As always you are stuck to books. Come, let's go,' Kalki said and we both left the store. We could maintain formality only for some time and then she said, 'Let's sit somewhere.'

'Yes, let's sit, I'm hungry too,' I said. There was a Café Coffee Day in front of us.

'I will take something for you and then let's go home. I'll make tea for you,' she stepped towards CCD to buy a sandwich.

'Hey, wait I'll get it,' I said, synchronizing my steps with hers and trying to reach the counter first.

'Shut up. Stay there and don't try to lead me,' she took out her wallet and said, putting her finger on the menu card, 'One cheesy veg croissant and one tex-mex-veg cheese sandwich.'

'So cheese is the secret of your health,' I teased her.

She punched me on my arm. 'I won't eat; this is all for you,' she took the packet and paid.

I laughed, 'Oh really. Then how did you get the enviable 80 plus?'

'Oh please! I'm not 80 plus. By the way, I'm dieting,' she smiled like a newly married bride. She kept the change in her wallet and we moved to the exit of the mall.

After walking for almost fifteen minutes, we reached her place. 'Good evening, how are you?' she asked the security guard, pressing the lift button.

The guard looked as if he hadn't eaten since the last few days but still smiled and said, 'I'm good.' The lift arrived and we reached the twenty-ninth floor where we got off and she unlocked the door.

The way she managed her home was unbelievable. I entered the hall. There were small lamps glowing on the window in a row, few around the sofa and one on the table with a couple in a dancing pose. There were old brass showpieces hanging on the front wall. I liked the deer neck with long horns. 'Would you like to have tea?' she walked in to the kitchen.

'Anything, but I need a glass of water first,' I stood up and followed her.

'Take it from the refrigerator.'

I opened the water bottle, had a few sips and sat in the sofa in the hall.

She came with a cup of green tea.

'I'm not on a diet,' I looked at her with a square face.

'Okay, do you want coffee?' she stood up.

'I'm just joking. It's okay,' I took the cup. We talked about Pakhi and a lot of other things during that hour. She lit one more lamp and kept it in front of Lord Ganesha. 'Come here and see,' she slid the window.

Kalki was standing to my right and we both were looking at the lights, local trains and cars, which were stuck in traffic. Everything seemed so beautiful from there.

'Whenever I feel alone, I come here and stand for hours,' she said. Both of us were standing there, placing our chins on the railing of the window.

She continued, looking somewhere outside, 'When my Nani left me, it was very difficult to live alone and manage everything because I didn't know anything about how to run a house. Now I manage my office...life is so good.'

She tried to support me. Her words had a lot of pain. She was well renowned and successful but somewhere there was pain in her heart. I was just listening to her and realized that I had already lived through the situations she was describing. More than twenty minutes passed and we were standing there and then I could see her wet eyes.

'Hey what happened?' I asked.

'Nothing...' she said, looking far away into the horizon.

'Tell me, what happened?' I wiped her tears. For a moment, I could see a glimpse of Pakhi in her.

'Hey, everything is fine now, don't worry. It's a part of life,' she said, wiping away her tears. A female heart is so kind and emotional that the love for others always trumps everything—regardless of whether she is running a house or a business.

Her left shoulder touched my right shoulder and I shivered and felt like I was losing my senses. I felt that after a long time I had met someone who could understand me, who could support me and who could replace Pakhi in my life. I came closer to her and my cheeks touched her shoulder and then I hugged her from the back tightly. My hands were on her neck, her left cheek was on my shoulder and I could feel her warmth. She pushed me back. The lights were dim and life seemed comfortable for a moment.

'Anuj! Stop it,' she urged. I hugged her tightly and our lips met for a moment. The moment that happened, I came to my senses. *What the fuck am I doing?* I paused and let her go suddenly.

'Stop it, Anuj. What is wrong with you?' She started crying and ran to the washroom. I was still thinking of what I had done a minute ago.

'How can I do that?'

'Am I a male slut who came here and kissed someone else?' Everything blacked out for a moment and I regretted my folly. I fell on the sofa, placing both my hands on my forehead. 'I have ruined our friendship.' I rubbed my lips with my handkerchief multiple times. I felt like I would puke. I took the water bottle, gargled and had some water.

I was sitting there on the sofa with my eyes closed. I didn't want to open them because I had done wrong and cheated myself—I had realized that the moment it had happened.

I could hear Kalki crying in her bedroom and that made me cry too. I was the one who had wronged her so I stood up and entered her room. She was sitting on a stool and crying helplessly. She was feeling violated. She ignored me and didn't even look at me.

'I'm sorry,' I said, standing in front of her.

'I trusted you and called you to my place and you did this. I never thought this could happen; otherwise, I'd never have called you. It's entirely my mistake that I trusted you,' she broke into tears.

'Please, just go away. I was wrong in calling you home. Just go away now,' she said and these words insulted me but I deserved that. My eyes were red with tears. I left at once. I knew I had made a mistake and I was embarrassed and lonely. I ran from there to forget everything but running from truth doesn't change it. The whole incident played out in my mind repeatedly. I couldn't sleep that night and I had one question to ask myself—how had loneliness overruled my self-respect?

I didn't have the courage to call Kalki again to say sorry, because sorry was not the solution for what had happened. I knew that nobody would understand how it felt when you are completely alone. That was a nightmare for me and life had already made me a male slut...

Why do you make me cry, you have left me so alone,
I have no one; only your memories are my own.

Are They?

$\mathcal{I}$ was dull and lethargic, was rolling around in my bed but didn't want to get up because whatever had happened yesterday had left me wanting to hide my face somewhere. I was fidgety and full of self-loathing thinking about that. The alarm had already snoozed thrice earlier and I finally left my bed.

Neither did I have any breakfast nor did I stop at Rahim Chacha's stall at the bus stop. He looked at me and smiled but I didn't react.

I had started discussing many things with him but that day I didn't want to discuss anything with anyone. I ignored him, caught my bus, and left for office. The expressions on his face were enough to show what he felt. Even in the bus and at the office I remained silent. Thinking about that the whole day, sitting in my chair, dusk came and within a few hours, my wristwatch said 8.00 p.m. In the bay of one hundred and fifty resources, only seven remained.

When people in America were having breakfast in the morning, we were sitting in front of computers to serve them. I stood up and went to the glass window to the left of my desk. I pulled down the curtain cord and looked at those who were smoking while standing outside at the road.

'Let's go downstairs,' Deepak sing-songed as he came to Yash's desk, wearing his jacket.

Deepak was the guy who always came late to office but every evening he was on time at the beer table. He was a software developer with three years of experience in the industry. He guided me several times on how to tackle situations or to impress the boss and they worked magically and I got some appreciation but later I got to know of some nasty things about him and stopped listening to him.

'I have a client call after fifteen minutes, so let's go now,' Yash replied.

'We'll come back in fifteen minutes,' he said and continued, 'Hey, did you attend the last session in conference room 31?'

'No, I was busy,' I answered, coming out of the bay.

Yash said, pressing the lift button, 'By the way the best thing about these brown bag sessions is that you can stare at that female instructor for an hour, measure each and every part of her body and nobody is going to stop you.' We all laughed standing outside of the office premises. He bought two cigarettes from a small kiosk and as usual one chewing gum for me.

Deepak and Yash lit their cigarettes holding it between the lips, while we stood in a triangle. He took a long drag and said, 'There is always a hole, just you need to put your ass on that to be an asshole and Bansal is such a big asshole.' Releasing smoke circles in the air, Deepak poured abusive water on his burning tongue.

'But what happened?' I asked him, though I knew the reason was that he didn't get an opportunity to work on the client side.

Deepak replied bitterly, 'That bloody bitch Bansal isn't giving me an opportunity that I deserve and want. Every dog is faithful but not every boss.'

All of us laughed raucously.

'Have you ever looked at Ambali? She always speaks in front of Bansal and tries to impress him. She doesn't know anything and at the end of the year she'll get better rating than us. That fucking Bansal thinks she's so intelligent,' Deepak was agitated now. He lit a second cigarette and Yash did the same.

'Let's go, have to finish some work,' I said, taking a long breath. I was getting bored with the same conversations every day. We walked to the lift and came to the bay. Whenever I felt polluted, I remembered the words of Rahim Chacha and that motivated me. He had told me—Feel happy about the work you do and if success comes then take it as reward and if it doesn't then take it as a learning experience for the next task.

'Are you not leaving?' Ambali asked me. Ambali, a perfect girl with blue eyes and green flecks in the irises. A kind expression, pretty smile, pink lips—those were enough to make anybody go crazy. Her curves were enough to entice all the men in the morning when she entered the bay. Her cute face was pretty as if she had been made only to support such a perfect structure. Yes, the moles on her neck, just below her right ear, always made her different from other girls...three moles in a triangle had made her famous in the bay.

'No, will leave in sometime, have to fix some code issues,' I replied, looking at my computer screen as I had been doing from the last twenty minutes without turning my neck.

Why doesn't anybody talk to her about her dresses? I thought. Every day she looked like a model when she entered the bay. Usually she wore deep-necked kurtis, inspiring the guys to use the washroom. From heels to matching nail paint, from earrings to pink coloured bras, Deepak and Yash had researched everything about her. Whenever she bent down to pick something or during the morning calls, they made a complete erotic visualization in their mind and narrated it during evening tea.

'See you! Have a happy weekend,' she said and walked towards the exit. Deepak ran to my desk, with his bag hanging on his shoulder and murmured, 'Look at her SSBA.'

'What is SSBA?' I asked. This was something new I had heard after my college days.

'SSBA means Shakira Shaking Big Ass. Deepak and Yash named her last week.' Yash looked really happy as if he had achieved something great that day and continued, 'God, just give me one night and an extra dotted condom.'

'Go and have Viagra first,' I laughed.

'Get lost,' he made a face and turned.

'See you guys on Monday,' Deepak and Yash left the bay.

It was so strange…we coded and delivered defect-free products to clients but we could never solve the puzzles of our own life. We delivered releases with quality without failing any deadline but we couldn't pass smiles to others. People like us had a good bank balance but that money was spent on treatment of hypertension and depression. They were so punctual in reaching office on time but they were always late on the dinner table. They always attended all morning calls but never called in the evening saying, 'Hey baby get ready, we'll go for movie tonight and then have dinner outside. So don't cook my favorite food at home.'

Are they happy with their wives? Are they happy with their sex life? Are their wives not sleeping with someone else who has time for them? Are their sons and daughters not doing drugs?

Moreover, at the end I asked myself, 'Are these equations wrong?' I never tried to find those answers.

'Hey workaholic, turn off your computer, go back home. It's late,' Payal interrupted my train of thought and said.

'Just wrapping up, I'll leave in some time. Are you going? Well…happy weekend with Sagar,' I turned my face to her and asked, rubbing my eyes. Her lips stretched into a big smile. Payal was working hard as she told me that, after reaching the next level, she would join the same company where Sagar was working and then they will move towards a happy married life.

'See you on Monday,' she waved and left the bay. I felt tired sitting alone in the office. I desperately needed a cup of coffee to keep my eyes open because I still had two hundred lines left to compile. I locked the computer and stood up, stretched my body as much as I could to relax and walked to the cafeteria. Crossing the glass wall cabins and bays, looking here and there, I could find only few remaining victims of the IT industry.

It was late, almost 10.30 p.m. To hide from the others, I took an alternate route to the cafeteria where only few cabins were in use. I crossed bay 13, 12, 11, 10, and 9, and then took a right turn towards the cafeteria. I could hear a metallic sound, some voice and something that I hadn't hear in the office before. I was scared for a minute. I retreated a few steps and checked three consecutive cabins. I took my cell phone out from my pocket and moved a step ahead trying to look inside conference room number 22 from the narrow strip-coated glass wall. I was confused and then I strained my eyes to see what was happening.

I was shocked and a cold chill ran through my legs. I felt like someone had snatched my soul from my body. I came closer to the corner of the wall and looked inside, raising my neck as high as I could. *What the hell is that?!*

The Hidden Truth

*S*he told me she was going home, then what is she doing here?'
I couldn't believe my eyes and shoved my phone in my pocket.
She was the one person I trusted the most. I saw Payal sitting in
the chair just next to her boss Bansal. She took some water from
the bottle and put it on the table. Bansal held her hand, saying
something that I couldn't hear. She pushed her chair a bit far away
from him and then he grabbed her shoulder in his hands and
then turned the chair around and pulled it in between his chair
and the front table. I looked here and there. What was going on?

Should I knock on the door? I thought. I moved a step and then
saw Payal kissing him on his left cheek.

What the fuck? Next moment I was in hell. He came closer to
her. They were in between the chair and the table, face-to-face,
and he started rubbing her cheeks and lips with his fingers. She
put her hand on the back of his neck. He suddenly put his hand
on her neck and then shoulder. She closed her eyes and raised her
neck like she was lost in a dream.

I was losing my mind and my eyes were red but I wanted
to know the hidden truth of this innocent girl who was my best
friend. The girl who was getting married to someone else was
here with another man.

I just looked at them. They started rubbing their lips on each
other's necks. He pulled the collar of her shirt and put his teeth
in her neck.

She unbuttoned the first button of his shirt and placed her

hand on his chest and he pulled her neck to his lips jerkily. He slid his hand to her butt, and tried to unhook her jeans but she held his hand to stop him.

He pulled her up and they stood up. She took the support of the table and he stood in front of her, locking her in his arms. He put his right hand around her waist and she raised her neck up, and he started kissing on her neck again. He took his shirt off and undid two more buttons of her shirt and tried to kiss her stomach. She stopped him and then he ran his hand on her back and waist. They hugged each other tightly. He slipped open the top of her dress almost completely, revealing her breasts and erect nipples. He grabbed her left breast in his hand and with the other he pulled her head, her lips to him. They kissed passionately. He bit her bottom lip gently and then nipped her neck, as he dropped his right hand down the middle of her breasts, down the front portion of her shirt and finally, falling between her legs, right where she wanted him so badly. Then she began to unbutton all the buttons of his shirt. He unhooked her jeans. They were almost naked. They pressed their bodies against each other. She put both her palms on the table with her body in front of him. She pushed him against the chair. He kicked the chair and it went far away. He pulled her to him very aggressively.

She sucked and kissed his collarbone and along the bottom of his stomach and went lower and lower. He grabbed her by the hair as she began slowly run her tongue up and down to his stomach and a bit lower. He pulled her up and unhooked her bra. She pushed his hand and then he stopped. She took her shirt and just tried to cover herself but all those buttons were still open. He shoved his hand into her jeans and she raised her neck as she moaned. She pushed him back and kissed him hard. They were lost in each other and then she put her hand in his pants and went deep.

He pushed her down on the table and ran his tongue on her back from neck to waist. He locked her stomach in his arms from the back. At the next moment, he pulled her jeans down a bit and started kissing her thighs. As she began to squirm and squeal, he put his thumb in her mouth. She started taking long breaths and moaned. She turned. Her eyes were on the ceiling as his head was on her stomach. She stroked his hair as he put his fingers in her jeans. She put her teeth on his neck and bit. She dug her nails in his back as he thrust her body across the table. She said something and then he took her hand and put it back down his pants.

She screamed in ecstasy. She left her hands there for a while and then both felt relaxed and comfortable. She looked at him in amazement as he pulled out of her, then smiled at him. They hugged each other and kissed.

It needed a lot of courage to ignore whatever I had seen. I could have called the security or anybody but neither did I call anyone, nor did I say anything. Once again, I looked through the glass with wet eyes. Dark clouds were shadowing my heart. Everything seemed like a void. I came back to my desk, took my bag and left that place...forever.

That was my last day in the office and of my friendships. I just forgot everything and never thought about it ever again.

The world is happy, they eat and they sleep,
I'm the only one, who wakes up and weeps.
Right becomes wrong when I open my eyes,
Life seems over and I feel like dying.

Some Sound Advice

$\mathcal{I}$ felt so alone, helpless and depressed, as there were only hurdles to cross in my life. I could feel the pain of an orphan girl when nobody looked at her. I could feel the pain of a baby boy when someone broke his favourite toy intentionally.

'When nothing works, listen to your soul's advice,' my mother used to say whenever I was confused or stuck in life. A ray of light is enough to remove the darkness but I felt like a blind person. I just hated that girl. I had no more feelings for her, whatever reasons she might have had for doing what she did.

Is life really this painful or am I the only unlucky one who is facing all this? I cursed my destiny.

But Rahim Chacha said everything happens for a good reason. Where is the good in all this? I trusted Payal and she... Did that happen for a good reason?

Every day I worked so hard and nobody said even a few words of appreciation to me, did that happen for a reason?

I'm struggling in my search for Pakhi. I don't know where she is; did that happen for a good reason?

That old man lied to me. I ran from the office and started walking down the dark streets with tears in my eyes.

'I will have to ask him,' I felt tired, empty. My face was yellow and lips were dry.

'But how can Rahim Chacha help me?' I thought. 'Whatever...I just want to meet him.' I ran towards the next signal to catch an autorickshaw for Rahim Chacha's tea stall. It was very late but I expected him to be there as he used to close his stall after 11.00 p.m.

I really needed to meet him in this situation. 'Andheri east,' I told an autorickshaw driver. He looked at me, nodded and pulled the rickshaw meter up. Sitting in the rickshaw, I looked at those who were walking on the road, the shops of vegetables along the road, a group of labourers with wrinkles on their faces who were coming back from work and at the last my eyes fell on a few couples holding hands, before the driver asked, 'You live in Andheri, saheb?'

'Why?' I asked loudly. 'That's not your business,' I added.

He smiled, looking at the side mirror, 'No, I've dropped you at your office many times so I asked.'

Oh! He knows me, I thought and nodded. 'Yes, I live there.' A teardrop fell on my hand and I squashed it with my other hand. He took a turn from the bus stop from where I used to catch my bus.

'Stop here, stop here,' I tapped on his shoulder. I looked at the meter, it said eighty-five rupees. I gave him a hundred-rupee note and started crossing the road. 'Your fifteen rupees,' he said waving a ten-rupee note.

'Thanks for driving so fast,' I waved.

'Where is Rahim Chacha?' I asked the small boy who used to sit there polishing shoes in his hut with his father. We rarely talked to each other except once when I had borrowed his pencil to write numbers of buses.

'Today is Friday so he left early,' he replied very politely and looking at my shoes he continued, 'But I can polish your shoes. They seem old and dusty.'

'You don't go to school?' I asked, crouching down on my knees.

'No, I don't go to school but I study mathematics here only,' he smiled and showed his mathematics notepad to me. I could see some sums and subtraction of numbers on it. 'But I can polish your shoe,' he asked again. I touched his cheeks softly. 'No, it's fine. You are not made for that. Do you know where he lives? Can you give me his address?' I stood up.

'Keshav is my good friend, we both play cricket together every day but he didn't come today,' he said, as if he hadn't heard what I asked for.

'Who is Keshav?' I was eager to know.

Rubbing his eyes, he replied, 'Rahim baba's son.'

'Can you give me his address?' I asked him again. He looked confused and searched for something in the rack behind the heap of shoe soles. 'Someone came today in the evening and gave this letter for him. Don't take it, else Baba will shout at me, but you can copy it from here.'

I smiled, 'Okay.' I almost snatched the letter from his hand and felt slightly better. 'Thank you so much my friend.'

'No, stop, give it to me,' he shouted excitedly. 'I'll write it for you,' he took his new pencil, sharpened it and gave me a naughty smile.

'Your handwriting is very good,' I smiled and took out a fifty-rupee note from my wallet and gave it to him. 'Keep this and don't waste it on useless thigs. I'm giving this so that you can buy yourself a notebook. And I want something in return.'

He looked at my dusty shoes and asked, 'What do you want in return?'

'Just your smile,' I pinched his cheeks.

'Bieee...' he said. I waved and headed for Dharavi. Dharavi is a heart-shaped settlement in central Mumbai. Sandwiched between Mahim in the west and Sion in the east, it is Asia's largest slum. Rahim Chacha used to live there.

After catching a local train for Dharavi and walking some distance, I reached those narrow streets of vegetables hawkers, very small fruit shops and vada pav stalls on wheelbarrows.

A girl was playing in the street wearing a torn frock. I preferred to ask her, as children are the best informers. 'Where does Rahim Chacha live?'

She looked at me from head to toe and then said, 'Just go straight, the last house is his.'

'Okay,' I thanked her and after walking straight could see an antiquated house. I had never visited these narrow streets earlier. I was a little scared.

I found my way to an unpainted door which was broken at the corners and looked many years old.

It was dark there except for a zero watt bulb glowing at the first door from where I had entered the street and that was far away now. I knocked on the door. Creaking and groaning at the hinges, it opened. Someone had opened the door but there wasn't enough light to recognize who it was, so I took some time. 'Oh you're here, come...come.' He recognized me immediately.

'How did you find my house? Welcome to my old shelter,' he smiled and welcomed me. I responded with great pleasure, respect and a smile, though I was suffering from inside.

'I wanted to talk to you but you weren't at your stall.'

He laughed with his old but pleasant voice. 'I am an old man, what do you want to talk to me about? You're always welcome here,' he patted my back.

Both of us sat on the cot. A small oil lamp was hanging on the right wall of the room. The paint was weathered and peeling off in spots, and the shutters on the windows were mostly broken. A slight breeze made the shutters tap against the hose and the hinges squeaked. The dim light from outside the window illuminated the room somewhat. I could hear a low moaning sound, perhaps nothing more than the wind blowing down the lopsided chimney.

'Oh! One second,' he stood up and took a glass of water from the earthen water pot and came to me. 'You must be thirsty.'

I took the glass of water, took few sips. 'Thank you,' I said.

His eyes were kind, his voice was clear and he seemed happy with my arrival. There was love in his words. A child emerged from the room.

'Say hello,' Rahim Chacha said with a glow on his face. I was reminded of my conversation with the boy an hour back when he had told me about Keshav. *Is that him?* I thought.

'Who's he?' I asked him to confirm.

'He is my brave son Keshav. I was narrating a story to him when you knocked on the door,' he held him in his arms.

'Keshav beta, you talk to Anuj while I make tea for him,' Rahim Chacha said and walked to his kitchen. His son reduced the light of the lamp and closed his notebook that was lying on the corner of the cot.

'Does he live alone? Where is his mother?' I enquired, looking around the room. There was something else that aroused my curiosity—the Gita and the Quran at the same place in front of a small calendar of Lord Shiva and Ganesha.

Har manzil kabhi apni si toh kabhi begani si lagti hai,
Yeh duniya tere hone ke baad bhi anjani si lagti hai.
Khuda bhi afsos karta hoga tere mere rishton par,
Yeh hindu aur muslim ki kahani hi ajeeb lagti hai.

'Who kept this here? Gita and Quran...' I asked Keshav. He smiled just like his father. 'Baba believes in the Quran and I believe in Lord Shiva and Ganesha. Baba says—nothing matters, all are the same.' What he said was unexpected from a child, thoughtful and true. I felt proud to be there.

'What happened?' Rahim Chacha put his cup on the table and asked.

He offered me toast. 'Nothing,' I said.

'How is your life going?' he asked very normally, sipping some tea. My eyes were wet and full of tears now. I wiped tears from my cheeks and said, 'Fine.' He took the cup from my hand, put it on the plate and asked, placing his hand on my forehead. 'You can tell me. I'll surely help you,' he said very politely. I held his hand as tightly as I could and closed my eyes. He took my hand in both his hands.

'Life is so difficult to live, so painful to survive and so bitter to know about and now I feel alone. I miss my memories,' I just said and then nothing came out apart from tears from my eyes.

Silence in the room made the words more effective. 'Don't cry, my son.' He wiped my tears. When he touched my cheeks to wipe the tears, that moment made me remember the time when Pakhi used to do the same when I was sad or my mom when I got hurt playing cricket in the streets and that made me cry even more. Those injuries were painful but now life seemed more hurtful. He smiled and said, 'Don't worry about that, that's not new—we always consider our present painful when we miss our old times when we were happy.'

I interrupted, 'I left my job.'

∽

He paused for a while and that positivity on his face was no more. He looked into my eyes, 'Why?' He seemed shocked but not scared, as I was 'Why did you leave your job?'

I couldn't reply and remembered all that had happened a few hours earlier in the office. 'My life is like a rolling stone on the way of this cruel world where only I'm hurt,' I murmured.

He sat next to me, 'Then there is no point in thinking about it. Never forget where the rolling stone gets its beautiful shapes from. So, what was the reason?'

'Nothing...' I didn't want to tell him why I had left.

'But there is always a reason. So tell me, what was yours?' he asked again.

'Nothing happens for a reason. You lied to me, everything you said was wrong.' I broke down and shouted in a pained voice, 'Nothing happened, nothing. I left my job. I didn't have anyone, I got a few friends and...I know I'm alone.' I felt the darkness around me, and feared that it would soon swallow me. I buried my head in my hands and rocked back and forth, sobbing as I did so, the tears streaming down my face. He sniffed and I wrapped my arms tightly around myself in a hug, hoping to comfort myself and put my head on my knee. My cheeks were stained with the endless stream of tears. I closed my eyes tightly and coughed and felt tears in my throat. I was rubbing my palm and regretted shouting at him. Keshav took the oil lamp from the stool and kept it in a corner of the room.

I turned and hugged him tightly.

'Don't cry. Don't cry. I won't ask the reason. Don't worry, you will find happiness soon,' he hugged me more tightly and patted me on my back.

'I'm sorry. I shouted at you. I'm really sorry,' I begged him.

He touched my chin, pulled it up a bit, and looked into my bloodshot, wet eyes. 'Whatever you said was your anger. Life is so beautiful, just look at it.'

'But all that glitters is not gold,' I said.

'But sometimes those are enough to throw light on the path that goes to your destination. Now wash your face. I've cooked some rice. Have some if you don't mind.'

'Why would I say no?' I said. He smiled and left for the kitchen. It was already 11.00 p.m. and I was quite hungry. I stood up, tucked in my shirt, walked to the basin and washed my face. He put the cooker on the floor. Keshav placed a mat and three plates in a row. That was the first time I experienced the flavour of two religions, two cultures and a pleasurable moment on a plate...the love of the Gita and the Quran.

I could see that deep happiness on his face when he said, 'Everyone's life starts and ends with open hands, but it depends upon you, how many times you make the V (victory) sign with your fingers and show it to the world during this journey.

There is no importance of sweetness without some bitterness, there is no importance of good without evil, there is no importance of love without hatred and there is no life without the truth of death. Your thoughts define how you live, so just live your life the way you want. We don't care about the present and spend precious moments missing our past. If we care enough about the present, it shall not become the past.'

'How do you know?' I asked.

He said, wiping his hands, 'Wait.' He tied a sacred thread on my right hand. There were a few old books on the table. I was turning the pages of one of these books when I saw a photograph of a well-dressed woman with two girls against a well-painted wall in the background. I wanted to ask him about her but felt awkward and decided to ask him the next time.

He unlocked the door and walked with me till the first corner of his street where a small bulb was glowing.

'Don't worry and always smile. Once you get back your Pakhi, I have many surprises for you.' He waved as I left.

I always trusted him and according to him, my happiness was on its way.

'I am going home tomorrow but what will I tell mom and dad?' I thought as I packed my bags.

An Indian Family—Sweet and Sour

Though I had no plans for the future because nothing happened according to plan, I thought it was better to live with family. I believed that there was happiness on the way but what was I going to do about those questions that neighbours and others were going to ask—What do you do? Where do you work? Last time Sharma aunty had asked about my age and investments and I had answered her proudly but what will I tell her now?

In India, we care about others' lives more than our own. Sometimes it made me feel special when Mrs Sharma brought a big bowl of gulab jamuns or dahi vadas or her special idls for me, but sometimes it was irritating when Mr Verma arrived early in the morning to read the newspaper at our place and get a cup of tea free with that. I suddenly smiled as I was reminded of the incident when the maid had shouted at him as he had forgotten to take off his slippers and had dirtied the floor.

I was going back with some happiness and some hesitation in my mind. It was 5.30 a.m., lying on the lower berth of the Rajdhani, I was thinking about my days at home. It was still quite dark as the sun was yet to rise. I woke up completely when I heard a guy who was on the phone with his girlfriend. I heard him murmuring, 'Baby, it's been a long time we haven't met, now I'm coming to meet you, are you not excited? Then come to me, I want to love you...please come to me...hmm... What are you wearing...I am also in a T-shirt and shorts... Okay, lift your T-shirt up. I just want to kiss you... Just feel me, I'm kissing there. My palm is now on your breast, just feel me… Give me your hand…and do something. I want to feel you today… Keep holding and don't stop…I can feel you…I love you… Which flavour do you like… but I like strawberry… Okay one strawberry and one chocolate with extra dots. Stretch your legs, baby…don't stop…'

Before I could kick his ass, the service boy came to take the order for morning breakfast. 'Hope they are done, bloody hell!' I was irritated.

I reached home in the afternoon. Meera and Payal had already called me multiple times. I messaged Meera that I had come home just to meet my parents and blocked Payal from my cell phone forever.

Meera messaged me: 'At least you could have informed me before you left. Anyway…it's not a problem, but listen, please bring aam ka aachar and besan ke laddoo when you come back and bring enough to last me a month. :P'

∽

Dad never showed his happiness on having me home but he brought my favourite fruits and told mom to cook my favourite palak paneer and woke me up early in the morning to go for a morning walk with me. He was my idol from childhood when he used to teach me geometry and Sanskrit. I wanted to tell him that I would always follow his path. However, there was a strange gap in our relationship. I always wanted to hug him and just wanted to share my feelings, but when I was a kid he never gave me the opportunity, and when I grew up I didn't have the courage.

'So how is the food in Mumbai?' asked mom while grating carrots and mawa in the kitchen. That was the best place ever to have a conversation with her. When I was a kid I used to sit on the slab and help her cut salads, chop chillies and clean rice grains. Now I had grown up so I was standing just next to her. I used to hide myself in her the folds of her sari when my dad scolded me for spending too much time in the kitchen. Sometimes I got slaps on my cheeks too.

'I miss your weird dishes,' I teased her, peeling green peas.

'Let's wait and see what your princess will cook for you. You have grown this strong thanks to my weird dishes.'

'I love you, my strict lady.' I pinched her on her shoulder.

A mother has a great heart. She's the only one who listens to you when something goes wrong and everything is messed up. She's there to save you when you are stuck in life and confused about your decisions. She keeps you safe for nine months and when you come into this world, she becomes your shadow; but sometimes we switch off the lights and the shadow goes away.

'But be careful about our status in society. You live there and you must be meeting many girls, but be careful, we won't support you at every step,' she put the grated carrots in the pan to make halwa.

'Yes, but what if I fell in love with someone?' I liked to make my mother smile by being naughty. I put the bowl to the other side, took a knife, made it red on the flame and dropped a few drops of water on it. Mom snatched the knife from my hand as it sizzled, 'Stop it. What do get by doing this? Stop it!'

'Haha…mom, do you remember you slapped me when I accidentally burnt Mansi bua?'

'Yes I remember, that mark is still there on her hand,' she said, sprinkling khoya and dry fruits on the halwa.

'Give me some,' I said.

'Grow up, you are not a kid anymore,' she said.

'I'll be the same always,' I said happily. A son is always a son for his mother, doesn't matter how old he is.

'I don't know how you live there alone.' She turned and washed her hands in the washbasin. Even though we shared such a fantastic bond, I was scared to tell her about my pain and problems. For a moment I thought I would go back to Mumbai and join my office again. There was no need to tell her... The next moment I remembered everything and decided to tell her.

'I want to tell you something, mom,' I said, gathering courage.

'Yes, tell me,' she covered the pan with a lid.

'Come here.' I called her to the living room and we sat on the sofa.

'Yes, now tell me,' she looked excited. She expected that I had some surprise for because I always used to give her surprises in that way.

'I left my job,' I said in one breath and no words came out after that.

'What?' she said, shocked. Her expressions changed within seconds. She asked again, 'What did you say?'

'I've left my job. I wasn't happy.'

'Do you even know what you are saying?' she stood up facing me.

'I know, mom. I tried my best to be there but I couldn't make it possible. I'm sorry, mom.' I regretted telling her but it was necessary because she was the only one who could understand me.

'But sorry isn't the solution. Is it? Most of your friends are struggling to get a good job and you left one that you had. Why did you do engineering if you wanted to be unemployed? Do you have any idea what you have done?

'Look at me, what is your goal in life? Your dad works hard from morning to evening and we spent most of our savings on your studies and you just left your job.'

'Mom please...I wasn't able to live there...show off, back stabbing, cheating...I couldn't work there. I'm not made for that. I'll search for a better job,' I said, holding her hands.

'And what about those who are living...are they crazy?' she asked angrily.

She was in tears. I wanted to hold her, to wipe her tears. I stood up but she stopped me and without saying a word went to the bedroom, saying, 'You did the wrong thing.'

Dad entered the dining hall and asked, 'Where is your mom?', and then crossing the lobby, he entered the bedroom. I didn't say a word.

Sitting alone, I was thinking about what I had done when I heard some unpleasant words from dad.

'This is the result of your love and over-indulgence. He does whatever he wants. You never ask him what he does in life. I work from morning to evening in an office and he wants everything on a platter...shameless!'

I gathered courage to enter the bedroom. Mom had her hands on her forehead, tears were flowing from her eyes and dad looked at me with red eyes and anger but didn't speak.

Why am I alive to see my parents in trouble because of me? I'm the one responsible for this. Why did I tell her? I thought.

Standing at the door, I said, 'I'll search for another job in a few days. Please don't worry.'

I remembered that day when I had got a good job in Mumbai and when my dad celebrated that moment with me feeling proud because I was one of those rare sons in his group of friends who had got a good job.

He turned to me and looked as if I had insulted him in front of thousands of people. 'You sister is twenty-eight now. It might not bother you but we are worried about her marriage. Don't you have any responsibility? I won't be with you for your entire life. From the day you left home, you seem to have forgotten your family. Don't you remember the time when you left home for IIT-JEE preparation to Kanpur and every week your mother used to go there to meet you? When you were in depression for six months, your mother and not the girl for whom you are doing all this, was with you day and night, don't you even care for her? Is love everything for you? Are we nothing?'

His words hurt me but I didn't know what to say.

'Leave him alone. Don't shout, we've fulfilled all his requirements and wishes, now it's up to him what he does with his life. He's sensible enough to distinguish between right and wrong,' mom said tearfully.

'This has happened because you never question him,' dad shouted at her.

'So what should I do? Should I hang myself? From the last twenty years I'm just dying, first taking care of your family and now...' She sniffed. 'If I do anything good then nobody notices it and when something goes wrong, I'm the one responsible for it. He's your son, too; you can also guide him,' mom raised her voice and said, wiping her tears.

She was deeply hurt. I came near the bed, grabbed some courage and tried to make them understand. 'Please don't fight, and I won't let you down, believe me.'

I left, went to my room and lay down on my bed. I didn't know when I fell asleep but when I opened my eyes, mom was in front of me. 'Get up and have something, then sleep,' she sat next to me on the bed and put her hand on my forehead.

I remembered the time when she used to be with me in the hospital from morning till evening. When I was a kid, she used to oil my body in the sunlight. Life was so happy, there was nothing to think and worry about. I held her hand, pulled it to my cheeks, held it tightly and shrank back into my bed.

'What happened?' she asked me, taking my hands in hers.

'Nothing, just be here for some time, please.'

'I'm here with you, don't worry.'

'You are the best mother. Don't worry and trust me, I'll find something better. Just take care of dad; he's tensed. I promise I won't let you down. Just trust me,' I said, taking her hands to my cheeks. She didn't reply. 'Now get up and have something,' she patted my cheeks and left.

Every day wasn't as beautiful as I had planned before coming home. There were smiles on their faces but insecurity in their minds about my future.

Everything happens for a reason, I knew, but was this happening to make or to break me? I was scared...and then something unexpected happened. I got a call from Anushka...

Last Knotted Thread of Life

$\mathcal{B}$efore leaving home, I had spoken to Anushka and she had said that she had found some contacts from Hansraj College where Pakhi studied for three years and they could help me find her.

'Have you got any other contacts? Should I come there?' I asked.

'I'm trying. You go to Mumbai. I will call you once I get some information. Don't worry, God is with us. Something good will happen soon. Take care.'

I came to Mumbai once again, the city of dreams, with some hopes from life. I did not pick up any calls from my office colleagues. I didn't want to meet anyone.

I had not heard from any of the software companies for recruitment. However, I had saved some money that I could use for the next two months to survive. Days seemed like weeks and weeks seemed like months. Two months passed at this tortoise pace but I still didn't have a job. One evening, I was sitting in the balcony of my room. The sun was about to set and seemed like the kumkum of a beautiful woman. At that very moment, my cell phone rang.

It was dad calling, asking if he should transfer some money into my account. Sometimes it's not wrong to lie if it doesn't hurt anyone. Therefore, I lied. 'Dad, I got a job in a company with a good pay.' It felt good to say that I had a good job but those were only words and not the reality.

'You've done me proud, my son.' Dad was so happy and his

words made me feel as if I had cheated him. I regretted my lie but there was no option.

'Are you coming for dinner?' Vishal asked me. The idea of going out made me happy but when my eyes fell on my wallet on the table, I said, 'No, thanks yaar. You go, I just had a very heavy meal in the evening.' I had become an expert at pretending and lying but he was well aware of my situation.

'Should I repeat that word or you are coming?' he said.

'I really don't want to go. You go...and which word are you talking about?' I replied, scratching the paint from the wall.

'Mofos,' he said laughing.

I started laughing. 'What is that?'

'Mofos stands for mother-f*#$ers...let me come back, I have more for you.' He stepped out and closed the door.

Who says money doesn't matter? Who says it doesn't give you comfort? I knew the value of money. Only hunger knows the value of a piece of bread. I had already spent nights having fried chickpeas with water to satisfy my hunger before going to sleep; else, I vomited in the middle of the night due to stomach pain. These were few hidden truths which I never discussed with anyone.

∽

In the month of winter, a cup of coffee and four hands, cold breeze early in the morning and few promises to be with each other. Yes, the day had come that symbolized love. Not very big but very small acts of love that made our love special.

The day came, Valentine's Day of the year 2013. The day to renew marriage vows for married couples and the day to make their feelings stronger for lovebirds who were dreaming of a life together. It's not all about how many precious gifts and roses you get. It is all about how you spread love all around. Love can't be celebrated in a day. It has to be felt, trusted and promised forever.

It was painful because on every Valentine's Day we made

few promises to be with each other but now only her memories were with me...

Three years back on 14 February, Pakhi had set seven rules for our love in a diary while we were in the theatre, and I called it CUSTOMIZED RULES OF LOVE: RT3LSP, and those were:

1. Respect each other as individuals.
2. Time and dedication for each other.
3. Trust is a must.
4. There is no place for sacrifices but share grief with each other (Don't try to be smart...it's better we cry together. I have good cotton handkerchiefs to wipe tears.).
5. Lie but don't hurt (As you always lie to give me surprises but every time I catch you).
6. Shout but never leave the other alone (I have a right to shout but you can't leave me alone in any case).
7. Passion in love.

Then we kissed each other passionately for very long until she bit my lower lip and wished me a very happy Valentine's Day.

Things shall change, months shall pass but feelings and the spark of love will never die; such was my love for her. I was thinking about all those moments that I spent with her. Like every year, nothing changed on this Valentine's Day; I woke up early in the morning and wrote something for her.

'Why did mom say that she will not come back into my life? She has to come back. I'll have to go to Delhi. Hope Anushka will find something soon I'll meet her soon,' I thought and wrote some lines:

This heart touched your heart on Valentine's Day.
These lips touched your lips on Valentine's Day.
We kissed each other; we hugged each other,
No matter where we were...we just melted into each other.
Your voice made me happy and I heard a loving sound,

There was a special fragrance when you were around.
You made the sky so blue,
And every moment was full of glee.
I feel like heaven when I think about you.
My heart stopped breathing when I couldn't find you.
I water the rose of our love and it dries,
You look like a princess when I look into your eyes.
My eyes are wet but feelings alive,
I will love only you, till the day I die.

The clock on the side table said 6.50 a.m. and I had to leave to meet the manager of McDonalds. It was not a 'respectable' job and it might not be what my parents thought I would do but beggars can't be choosers. And moreover, no work is big or small. The last fifty rupee note in my pocket made my decision for me. Even I had not thought about it but life goes on and I had decided to follow the path it chose for me. People and society have their own views, but in the end they celebrate one who follows his heart. I didn't know how true it was but I had trusted an old man. People called him a tea maker but for me he was no less than a preacher. Rahim Chacha always supported me.

I smiled and headed towards the nearest McDonalds to enquire about the job. Just then I got a call informing me that I had been shortlisted for an interview with a company. Then I entered McDonalds, not for work, but to have lunch, but this time a delicious burger and a coke float. I had some hopes for tomorrow.

Next day, I reached the office where the HR manager was interviewing people and I was the third last person to enter her cabin. I was called and a peon came to direct me to the cabin. 'So why did you leave your previous company?' This was a general question but I didn't have the general answer. I just said that I wasn't getting good opportunities to work there. She looked at my wristwatch that had stopped in the bus; I had manually set it at 11.00 a.m., and from the last fifteen minutes, it was showing the same time. She smiled. I felt embarrassed but smiled back.

She turned a few pages of my file, asked a few questions about my technical skills, and said, 'You can join us from Monday.' I was in seventh heaven.

'Thanks a lot,' I said to her. I couldn't share my happiness with mom and dad as I had already told them that I had got a good job.

However, I was eager to meet Rahim Chacha and reached his tea stall. 'You look good in that white kurta,' I said.

'Haha...thanks...and you look good when you smile,' he said pouring milk and water in a pan.

'You want tea?' he asked, holding the kettle in his hand.

'Yes...yes, why not and that too with two spoons of extra sugar.' He looked at me with a big smile and his eyes wanted to know the secret of my happiness. He poured tea into a disposable cup. 'So, what's the reason for the two extra spoons of sugar?' he finally asked.

'Because I got a job and this is for you,' I had bought a white and blue shawl for him by borrowing money from my neighbour and promising to return it by the end of the month.

'For me?' Rahim Chacha asked, surprised.

'Yes, don't you like it?'

'This was not necessary, my son.' When tears of happiness fall from old eyes, that means you've done something worthwhile in your life. I felt the same seeing him.

He kept it in his bag. 'God is always with you. Keshav was asking about you yesterday and told me that you played cricket with him. Today is his birthday; if you come he'll be happy,' he offered me the tea and started packing his utensils. 'Now I have to go. He'll be coming from his school and if he won't find me at home then he will ask for chocolates and chocolates cause cavities,' he laughed, hanging his jhola on the handle of his cycle.

'Oh, that's great news. Am I invited to the party then?' I was excited and got a reason to celebrate.

'Of course, and if you come early then we can go masjid and then the temple too,' he smiled.

I went to stand in front of his cycle. 'May I ask a question, I don't know if I should ask or not but...'

He smiled as he always used to when he knew my question. 'I have never stopped you from asking anything and have always answered your questions, so ask me.'

'Masjid and temple...' Before I could say more, he answered, 'You asked the same question to Keshav. This is not the right time to tell you that. I'll tell you one day. Till then I've one answer for you—On one hand we talk about our ancient times and worship Brahma, Vishnu, Mahesh, Jesus, Mohammad and on another we talk about religion. Do we know the last names of Brahma, Vishnu, Mahesh, Jesus and Mohammad?'

His words touched my heart. 'You are great,' I saluted him.

'I never use my last name from the day I lost my daughters, my wife and my job just because I am a Muslim. Was I not human first? Were those Hindus not human first who didn't help me because I was a Muslim. That changed my life and...'

'What happened to them?'

'This is not the right time,' he smiled, paddled his cycle and left. 'See you in the evening,' he turned his head and said.

Now I was more curious to know what had made him like that. Whatever he had said about my life came true.

God never sends special creatures on earth; they become special with their deeds. He became my favourite teacher with no religion, no formalities and no demands.

That evening with them was one of the best evenings of my life.

Sounds of Silence

$\mathcal{N}$ow everything was changing very slowly. Life was like an oil lamp; though I was glowing, I was burning from inside. People congratulated me on small successes but I had lost the real nectar of life that was love.

Winter had gone in her romantic memories, summer had gone with dry days and now rains had come. It was early June when clouds started romancing around but rains were still waiting to hug Mumbai. Every day I used to sit on the seaside after work. There was a special bond that I could feel with those waves. The sky was clear and blue when I left for my office in the morning. I carried an umbrella without any reason because rains had stepped in at some other places in the state of Maharashtra. I had a special love for the rain as it washes out everything.

I was walking on the promenade along the road at the northern end of Marine Drive and then stood by the sea. The air was refreshing and the view was magnificent just after sunset. After sundown, everyone seemed to head for Marine Drive to get some fresh air at the end of the day. There were plenty of people sitting along the way and it was interesting to observe people simply from here. A long walk along that road reflects all that life throws at us. This road has two sides, one that goes towards all the corporate offices, workplaces, shopping complexes and hotels, and the other side, as we all know faces the sea. A simple observation reveals that during office hours on weekdays you see legions of people on the other side and nights give way to crowds on the sea face side. This is truly a time when people switch off the lights and come here to listen to their heart. People who listen to it know it from very close.

The sea, inadvertently, becomes a passive listener for all.

This was the place where I had spent the first eight months of my professional life. This was the place which had a lot of significance for me, as it was the only source of solace in my otherwise hectic and ruthless life. I was looking far into the sea, and then in a split of a second, it started raining. Those who were alone opened their umbrellas and couples preferred to get wet in the first rains of Mumbai. A couple was standing under an umbrella, enjoying the rains and romancing. I was just staring at them, standing far away from them. 'Why don't they enjoy the rain?' I thought. Rains were the mist that pattered above a quiet alcove. They brought the scent of wonderment and renewal.

I remembered something, something that already had changed everything in my life. I remembered when we were standing at Rajiv Chowk under the umbrella that night, she asked for an ice cream, and next morning we were both coughing but without any regrets as we had enjoyed together. Death seems so beautiful when you live together and love together for the whole life.

A romantic couple crossed me as they threw their umbrella and walked away into the rain. They looked like birds flying in an open sky with love and passion.

I preferred to close my umbrella too because still it was in search for its mate and without her it seemed painful to carry. I looked at the sky. The drops on my face were cool and refreshing, and seemed to stick to my eyelids. I closed my eyes and it felt good to cry when nobody could see me. Tears shall wash out with the rains and I prayed that a new season would come after these rains. I could listen to the sound of silence of my heart.

I feel alone and left out, full of sadness and loneliness.
Your absence is slowly consuming my life and killing my soul day
by day.
Is life all about suffering? Is life all about struggle?
Is life all about earning money and not happiness?
Am I happy without her? Is she happy without me?
Shall we meet again?

I stopped a couple of times along the way to take in the beautiful views of the skyline, the sea, the beach, couples, friends, families, and me...alone. The only way to cover my pain and survive was to keep smiling, find ways to cheer myself up and laugh out loud—this made me who I was. Restricting me from doing this felt like living in the desert all alone and killing myself slowly. 'I can hear you around me. I can feel you in the breeze, I want to see you,' I murmured, walking swiftly on the road with my eyes watering continuously. I just paused for a moment and looked at my feet, wet with tears.

I sniffed, wept and wiped my eyes. I started walking on this long road that was one of my favorite stress busters and bought a water bottle from a hawker and again sat on the sidewalk for a moment's relief.

It was tough but this place has something that takes your mind completely off your problems. It makes you reflect on larger, better and more beautiful things.

'What happened to you, my son?' an old, experienced voice dropped into my ears. I turned back. 'Oh, you're here. Nothing, I'm good.' I rubbed my eyes and gave him a smile.

'Yes, I'm here,' he smiled too and spread positive waves around me.

I looked at his cycle standing a few steps behind him, with two big kettles and one small bag that he used to carry hanging on the handle. Rahim Chacha left his cycle on the side and came to me. 'I come here on weekends.'

I welcomed him, 'Good to see you.' I was facing the sea and he came and sat next to me facing the roadside.

'What about you?' he asked, turning to me.

'I usually come here after office. I love this place. It gives me peace.' I added, 'Can we sit for some time, I want to ask few things about you. May I?'

'Yes, sure,' he smiled.

'Is there something special that you put in your tea?' I asked looking at the waves which were trying to be a part of our conversation.

'One spoon of extra sugar makes the day,' he laughed and patted on my shoulder. He stepped back as if he was afraid of waves.

'Tell me the secret of one spoon of extra sugar?'

He laughed.

Did I crack a joke or did I ask a stupid question? I thought for a while but I asked what I had wanted to for so many days.

'The secret is, a few minutes back, there were tears in your eyes and now there is a smile. Your words decide your nature and your nature makes you different from others. But I'm an old simple man,' he grinned.

'Rahim Chacha, don't play with me, tell me, who are you?' I requested desperately.

'Do you really want to know? However does it matter?' he raised his eyebrows and gave me a sarcastic smile. I never liked that.

'Yes, I want to know the truth. Moreover, why are you helping me? I don't know you. How and where do you come from whenever I cry? This is not a coincidence. Tell me who you are,' I raised my voice and he started laughing. 'Calm down.'

He started, 'Twenty years back, when I was young man, I used to come to this place with my children Ayaan, Akram and Razia, and Sultana—their mother and the best person on earth. We had a perfectly happy family. I used to work in a cloth mill at that time and was living a happy, prosperous life but everything changed in a day.

'It was Razia's fourteenth birthday. She was the only girl in our family. Every year we celebrated her birthday with all our relatives.

'It was Tuesday, 11 July 2006, when she went out for shopping in the evening with her brothers Aayan and Akram. The moment I came to know about the blast in the local train at Bandra, I called Razia and asked her to come home by bus. I was watching the TV and calling her as one by one the blasts happened in one local train after another and I could never call her again... The last blast happened in the Borivali local train and my entire family was in it. Within eleven minutes, I lost my children. I lost everything. I lost my world. Sultana couldn't bear this pain and suffered a paralytic attack. I fought till the day I could. Sultana was in the hospital for two months on oxygen twenty-four hours. She couldn't endure the pain of that tragedy. I was thirty-five years old that time. Whatever I earned, I spent on her medicines and treatment. After a month when I went back to work, I was informed that I was no longer a part of the mill where I had been working for the last three years. I asked about the reason for this but got no answers. Then I came to know from one of my co-workers that the manager had kicked out every Muslim from the mill. I waited for the manager in front of the mill the whole day. When he was leaving in the evening, I pleaded in front of his car. He gave me five thousand rupees, folded his hands in front of me and left saying that, 'I received an order from the top management and can't help you but keep this money. That is all I can do for you.

'After some days Sultana also left me.'

He sniffed and wiped his tears. 'This is the truth of life. Nobody waits for you. They just go away.'

'Who is Keshav then?' I asked.

'When Sultana left the world, I adopted Keshav. He was five years old that time and now he's eleven. Who knows better than me how life changes?' He broke down and continued after a while.

'Now I live only for him. When I reach home in the evening, we play, we eat and we enjoy our time together. I know how quickly life changes, I've faced it. You asked me about the secret of my smile, this is the secret. There are so many problems in our life. Nobody is completely happy. Everyone came here empty-handed and will go in the same way but what matters is how many times you make others happy during this journey. Life is all about living. Life is never perfect, you have to make it perfect.

'Just after three minutes of my calling my daughter, she left the world. You never know what will happen tomorrow. I learnt one thing from my experience: you can't change the past and you don't know about future, so it's better to live in the present.

'I have to go now. See you tomorrow at the bus stop.'

My wet eyes pleaded with him to say more. I saluted him. He paddled his cycle and went towards the other side on the way to his place. It was feeling sad after listening to his stories but also a little happy that, in last few months, I had come to know Rahim Chacha a lot more closely.

As I had promised Meera I would meet her, I didn't miss the 17.37 local from Marine lines to Bandra and messaged her that I was on my way. I wanted to tell her about Rahim Chacha as she had been asking about him for several days because she wasn't sure why he had helped me.

Thoughts over Coffee

$\mathcal{I}$ was late so buying chocolates was the best options to save myself from her scolding.

I was waiting for an autorickshaw and my cell phone vibrated. You should never argue with girls or women when they are waiting for you because they haven't been created to wait, they have been made to be pampered.

'Do you wear a wrist watch?' Meera asked over the phone as my mother used to ask me when I was out with my college friends.

'Yes, I do but today I forgot to wear it.' I knew what she was trying to do.

'Someone promised to meet me today. I think he forgot.'

'Someone is on the way, reaching there in ten minutes. I have something for you.' The autorickshaw was moving at a snail's pace in heavy traffic.

'That chocolate idea doesn't work every time. You are thirty minutes late.' Girls all over the world will remain the same always—sweet and spicy.

'I need your mercy, my lord. Just give me five minutes,' I replied teasingly to make her smile.

'Shut up and come soon.' The driver increased the volume of the song and coincidentally, the song was—'Bhaag Bhaag…D K Bose…D K Bose…D K Bose…Bhaag bhaag…D K Bose…D K Bose bhaag'.

He looked at me in the front mirror and smiled. He accelerated, wheeled towards Bandra west and dropped me in front of CCD.

Sitting alone in the corner, holding a glass of cold coffee with a straw in the corner of her mouth, she was reading a novel and just turned the last page when I entered CCD. A hairband in her silky hair made her look even more charming. She never wore heavy jewellery, bright hued lipsticks or kohl. Minimal make-up and just small diamond earrings made her so beautiful.

'When will you stop looking so gorgeous?' I murmured, sitting by her side.

'Hey,' she looked at me, gave a smile and added, 'how are you?'

'I'm good. You didn't answer. When will you stop looking so gorgeous?'

'Never,' she smiled, placing a bookmark and keeping the book aside. 'By the way, hot girls have coffee and smoking hot girls read books with coffee.' She laughed out loud.

'Yes, I know, apologies for being late.'

'It's okay. You would be dead if you had forgotten.'

'I know this doesn't work every time but there was no other way to save myself.' We both laughed as I gave her the chocolate. We were meeting after a long time but nothing had changed. We spent more than an hour talking about random things.

'So, after leaving that job, are you living your life happily as you wanted?' she asked. The one who gives strength to the world is the weakest person at heart, I felt. I didn't answer.

'So what do you do after work, when do you reach home?' she asked.

'Firstly, I never call it home. That is just a place where I live. I don't know. I usually don't map out my timings,' I said.

She looked around here and there and said, 'You go back to your place, work hard, plan things for the next day, have your dinner, watch TV, open your laptop, look at her old photographs, feel bad, shed tears, shout alone and sleep with your wet pillow. Where is the life?' I didn't answer as those questions didn't have any answers.

'Think about it till I get a coffee for you,' she said and stood up. The café guy was giving us questioning looks as we were just talking and hadn't ordered much.

'Hey, you sit, I'll get it. You girls are precious, I can't make you slave,' I joked.

'Oh please! Sit down, I don't believe in that and my friendship demands no formalities. I'll be right back.' She was smiling but I could see she was angry that I had left office without informing her. Life seems beautiful when great people are around. Life seems precious when you start liking those people. Firstly, Rahim Chacha came to my mind and then she. She always made me smile and feel happy. Thinking these sweet and sour thoughts, as usual my mind again thought something that it was not allowed to think. 'Do I like her?' I asked myself. Before I could answer, my heart said something, something for Pakhi:

I am breathing…I am breathing…I am just breathing for you.
I am listening…I am listening…I am listening to you.
Are you thinking about me? Are you listening to me,
wherever you are?
My heart searches, my mind thinks of you.
My legs bring me back, and I just cry for you.
I am waiting…I am waiting…I am just waiting for you.
I am waiting for your touch…I am waiting for your kiss.
I'll wait till the last breath.

I was lost in my thoughts. 'Hello!' she waved her hand in front of my face. I came out from my dreams. 'No! Nothing, thanks,' I held the glass of cold coffee.

'So…did you think about it?' she asked again but I didn't answer and then she continued, 'When you left that office, you could have called me once if you ever counted me in your life.' Girls are girls, they don't speak much but their body language speaks a lot about their feelings—she was hurt.

'You know everything, Meera. I wasn't in a situation to call you. Hope you understand,' I said.

'Well, leave it,' she smiled. I couldn't answer her previous question but I was still stuck on a few others:

Do people really meet again? Do we find that person for whom we live our whole life? Is it all about destiny?

Will Pakhi return to my life?

With a few sips of coffee remaining in our cups, Meera touched my hand. I ignored it the first time but the way she looked at me clarified many things. She liked me but since when, I didn't know. I also liked her, not because she was pretty, intelligent and a complete girl but because she was a very good person by heart.

I held her hands in mine and asked her, 'Do you love me? She was shocked and surprised but somewhere a smile reflected on her face. Girls don't walk around wearing their hearts on their sleeves, they take time. She took time to reply and then said, 'Yes, I do.'

Her eyes met mine. She ran her fingers in her hair and was very nervous.

'That's great. I'm so lucky. Let's go get married and run away from this world. What do you say?'

She had never expected these words from me. She released her hand and said, 'But you love Pakhi.'

'If you know this then why these feelings for me? Can't we be friends? I don't want to lose you because I've already lost many. It is true that I like you a lot as my good friend but a friend can't be a life partner. I just wanted to clarify that, and I respect you and your feelings.'

She nodded, took my hand and kissed it. 'You are stupid but a good friend and yes, a mad lover. Just take care of yourself. Don't curb the spark within you. I'm here to lift up the curtain just a bit. I'm always with you.'

She said the same words as I had said to her and laughed.

We both walked out of the café and started walking along the road.

'Why don't we hire a direct cab to your place?' I asked her. She slowed her steps and looked at me with a cute smile on her face.

'You don't like walking along the sea? Don't you like it when the waves touch your legs and try to hold your waist each time? Don't you like it?' Meera rose like a flower. She bent and folded her denims till her knees. She came right up to the waves. I didn't speak but synchronized my steps with hers and tried to feel the pleasurable touch of waves. *I want to smile. I want to laugh. I want to feel. I want to be happy. I want to live in these moments...but for whom?* I thought.

'Of course, for yourself, you have to live for yourself. Nobody lives for others,' she said. I was shocked because I hadn't spoken a word and she had guessed what I was thinking. It was dramatic but true. I took a small pebble and threw it in the sea with great force. I could not say anything after that.

'Never blame yourself. Never blame others. Good days give happiness and bad days make you mature and experienced. Good can be better but best is always the best,' she said.

'Oh, is it?' I laughed.

'Why are you hurting yourself, your family, your friends and your life?' she shouted, holding my hands in front of many people around us.

'I'm sorry, I didn't mean it but look, till when you are going to wait for her?'

'Till the day my heart hates her, I'll wait for her. I loved her truly, and I will wait for her. Look at the sea... It has nothing special in it but it calls us to come here every day and we feel peaceful when we are here. It holds numberless precious things in its embrace in the same way as I have those precious feelings and love for her. No matter when but she has to come, she has

to give me one reason for leaving me so alone...'
    She smiled, patted me on my back and we moved on our way.

Lose every battle of love but never look at yourself as a loser,
Look at yourself as a winner because you are one.

God Listens When You Call in Search of Yourself

It was just like any other day when I was browsing the Internet, sitting motionlessly in the chair after coming back from work. Soon the clock said 2.30 a.m. When married couples make love at night, the unmarried watch naughty American videos and help themselves; I was aware of this fact but was reminded of it when I heard some seductive sounds from Vishal's room…hmm…aahh…aahh…deeper…come-on…harder…don't stop…don't stop and then complete silence. This gave me a lot of food for thought and I was wondering what would happen to the world without these videos that provide such mental and physical satisfaction to the masses.

I got back to my work as I had a meeting with some American clients the next day.

After a long time I remembered my college days which I had forgotten in the fast running life of Mumbai. Those college days with friends and those romantic nights were no less than heaven where there were only two birds with a golden nest, the nest of love. I was missing those times badly; I stood up suddenly, took out my old denims from the cupboard and shoved my hand in its back pocket. There was a beautiful card in my wallet that Pakhi had given me on the last day of summer, when I was returning to college after spending one month with her in Delhi. On a gift wrapper on which she had written—'Times may be good or bad but I'm always with you'. Every morning before leaving for office or on any important day, I used to look at this message written on the gift wrapper and that actually motivated me. Those were a few physical things with me and rest were just her memories.

I took out everything from my old torn wallet from the other pocket of my denims—SIM card, memory card, a gold coin that my mom had given me on my birthday, a few ATM withdrawal statements, a photograph of mom and dad... I placed everything on the bed.

'Oh, there must be some money in my secret zip,' I thought cheerfully as I opened it. I always kept some money there to save it from friends or for urgent needs in my college days. Anyway, I didn't find anything apart from some old papers which I also placed on the bed with others things and threw some useless papers in the dustbin. I just started unfolding those papers just to clear my wallet and make it light. To give: Deepak-202, Naveen-178, Sumit-98, and Mohit-316. To take: Sanjeev-230, Rohan-110. I just laughed looking at that credit list of college days that was still to be settled.

I opened another. Every piece of paper was special and carried some rare memories. Then I realized that my wallet was actually expensive not because of the money but those memories. I unfolded one more paper. It wasn't shocking; it caused an tremor inside me. I threw the pillow somewhere and took out my cell phone. It was a photocopy of Pakhi's college ID. I just called Anushka and my body shivered with every minute that seemed very long until Anushka picked up the call.

'Hey are you at home?' I asked her in a hurry.

'No, in my bed with my boyfriend kissing and smooching him, and he just unhooked my...and then my phone rang...is there anything else you want to know?' Anushka said in a sleepy voice with her dirty mind still working at its regular pace.

'Hey, I got her address,' I said and ignored everything else.

'What the fuck...you got her address Pakhi, right?' she shouted excitedly and continued, 'Hey I was joking. There was a party at home, so I just came to my room. Forget that, tell me everything—How? Did she contact you? Did she read the book?' she asked all the questions in one go.

Staring at that address on the paper, I said, 'No, she didn't contact me. Three years ago when I went to her college, she took some zeroxes of some receipts and ID. She gave me the extra copy and I kept it in my wallet. To save it from others, I kept it in the hidden zip of the wallet because in college days, friends always asked for a treat and they used to take my wallet without permission.'

'That's her Delhi address, right?' Anushka asked eagerly.

'Yes but I folded it multiple times so I can't figure out what it says exactly but it's Surya Nagar something, I can't see the house number correctly.'

'Don't worry, come to Delhi, we'll find her. I'm so happy for you. Now just pray everything should be fine.'

'I'll be there tomorrow morning,' I just said without thinking further, without any confusion and without any deliberation because that day had come.

'It's 2.55 a.m. already. How will you come in the morning? Go and sleep properly, I will plan something till then.'

'Sure. Bye, good night. Sorry I woke you up in the middle of the night,' I said in a low voice.

'It's not midnight, it's 3.00 a.m. and you will have to pay for that,' she said and that made me smile.

'Sure, good night,' I disconnected.

I booked flight tickets for early next morning, washed my face with cold water and packed my bag in the next twenty minutes.

I left a note on the table for Vishal: 'Hey, leaving for Delhi. Nothing serious but just urgent, will tell you everything once I come back. You should say thanks to me that I didn't wake you up. Don't bring any girls in my absence to the flat...lol; I can smell them easily. So be careful, party hard, take care.'

I left for the journey I would remember forever and reached Delhi at 8.35 a.m. I was excited and nervous. I was scared of losing her but didn't know why. Taking the metro, I reached CP. I called Anushka.

'Hey, get up, I'm here at CP.'

'What the fuck? You've reached.'

'Yes.' I pressed the phone to my ear so that nobody could listen to her swear early in the morning.

'Why you didn't tell me that time? I'm still in bed. You're waiting at CP?' she said in a sleepy voice.

'Yes, and I know you'd be here in the next thirty minutes because Delhi girls are fast and furious. I'm waiting here at CCD, come soon,' I said, holding the menu card in my hand and thinking about Pakhi.

'Okay, I'm coming there.' She disconnected the phone call.

I ordered an Irish coffee and saw a couple fighting for a very stupid reason—why wasn't he wearing the shirt she gifted him last time…love is just like that.

Her hair was thick like satin and her jet-black curls blew softly in the morning breeze, and as they did so, they looked like the black waves that fill oceans on stormy nights. Her brows were soft, quizzical and serene with purity and wisdom. Her jaw was set and her mouth was chewing something—chewing gum or chocolate. Her eyes were deep as a great body of water and just as blue. They looked through you without fear as if they already knew what they were to find.

'There you are, Romeo,' Anushka laughed and entered.

'Why are you regurgitating?' I looked around as she laughed at me. Few of them noticed me, and that couple smiled.

'I'm not a buffalo, okay,' she punched on my right shoulder.

'Hey that hurts!' I said as she pulled up a chair and sat down. I gave her the coffee that I just ordered two minutes ago.

'Hey, thanks,' she said.

'You're looking good or I must say, a stunner. *Bas bhagwan ne thodi akal de di hoti toh mazaa aa jata.*' Most of the eyes turned and got stuck on her dimples. She raised her eyebrows and looked at me with her half-closed eyes. 'I'll kill you.'

Then she stood up, licked the drop of coffee on the corner of her lips and said, 'Let's go.'

We reached Anand Vihar by metro and took an autorickshaw to City Center Market, Surya Nagar.

'Are you sure we can find this address?' I asked her. I just wanted to hear an affirmative reply from her. It was my belief that in this beautiful life, we meet new people and sometimes we just meet the old ones again. I prayed I would meet Pakhi this time.

Sitting in an autorickshaw, she said, 'Hey show me that photocopy.' I shoved my hand into my back pocket and handed it to her.

'You are slightly late but so smart for keeping this safe,' she smiled and looked confident about finding that address. I kept my fingers crossed though that was only affectation to make me believe that everything would be fine. However life is not always as we think—it changes in seconds.

∽

'But it's not clear, it's washed out. I can't read it,' she said, staring at the paper without blinking.

'Yes, but it must be 9A or 8A.'

'Anuj, it's not 9A or 8A. It could be 5A or 3A.'

I looked outside and wished that two years ago, when we used to go in autorickshaws, I had dropped her home. It would have been so much easier to find her now.

We got off in front of a hoarding of the honourable prime minister near Anand Vihar. Looking at poor children who were sitting and eating something from a dustbin under that, she murmured, 'Our country.'

'Hey where are you going, we have to go,' I raised my voice.

'Just a minute,' she said, approaching them.

'You can only help them in burning this hoarding, you can't change the rest. Don't waste time and let's go we're getting late.'

She went there, snatched that small piece of bread from a child's hand and threw it back in the bin. One of them shouted on her, 'What are you doing with our food. Get lost.'

I laughed, looking at her. 'I told you.' She looked at me angrily.

'Don't eat this unhygienic food. Moreover, you look like the elder one amongst them, why don't you stop them,' she shouted.

'We live alone, they are my brothers and sisters, we live there.' He pointed to one of the slums situated next to the road.

'In that house?' she asked.

'No we don't have a house, we live there under that tree,' he replied.

She took a hundred rupee note and gave it to him saying, 'Go and buy something to eat but don't waste the money okay?'

'Mother Teresa...' I said and then ignored them.

The boy smiled. 'Thank you so much. I'll buy five oranges for us.'

She turned back and an old woman approached me. I felt awkward. 'All poor people live here,' I murmured. Anushka just came and stood next to me, that old woman said in very low and poor voice, 'I know you, and you gave me a ten rupee note in front of Anand Vihar metro station. There was a girl with you too.'

This time Anushka laughed.

She wants more money, I thought and said out loud, 'I don't have money now. Why don't you work?'

Anushka pushed me back and asked her in hurry, 'Yes, there was a girl and we're looking for that girl. Can you help us find an address?'

'Anushka, she's an old woman, she doesn't know anything.

What help can you expect from her?' I pulled her hand.

'Hey stop it. Stay here. Old people are not stupid; they're more intelligent than us.'

She asked something and the old woman guided her to A-block...

Knock at the Door

The old woman showed us the path we had to take. Everything seemed to be working in our favour, first that paper and then the old woman. Life is all about surprises, things never happen according to your plan.

'Love starts with spring and ends with autumn,' I murmured.

'No, true love starts with spring and grows more with autumn. We'll find her, don't worry,' she said and smiled.

We reached the address we thought was on that paper but somewhere in my mind, I wasn't sure that I'd knock at the right address... Life is not as simple as we think.

She stepped ahead a bit and asked about the address once again. There was a hope in my heart but I was also scared, what if I didn't find her? Looking at that nameplate, I rang the bell; nobody came. She rang the bell; nobody came. I rang the bell again and a girl opened the door.

I was nervous like a woman before giving birth to her child or a girl before entering at her in-laws' home.

'She must be her cousin,' I guessed.

'Hi, my name is Anushka and he's Anuj,' she said, pointing to me. 'Does Pakhi live here? We're her friends and have come to meet her.' I was standing behind Anushka. That girl looked at us for a while. 'I think you're at the wrong address. Nobody with this name lives here,' she replied.

'But she lives here only. Call her,' I shouted.

'Stop it, Anuj,' Anushka said.

'Is it the same address?' I gave her the paper, expecting she might be able to guess what was written there—9A, 8A, 6A, 5A or 3A.

'Yes, this is the correct address but nobody with this name lives here.'

'Do you know anyone with this name in the neighbourhood?' I asked her.

'I'm not sure, wait, let me ask my mother, she must know.' She called her mother. Her mother came to the door and the girl asked her if she knew anyone by that name.

'No beta, I have never heard of any Pakhi in this building. There are thirteen blocks in the society, and it's tough to find the one you're looking for. I could help you if you had the block number or at least the building number. Do you have the flat number or building number with you?' her mother asked me.

'No, we don't have it,' Anushka said in a low voice. 'Thanks aunty,' we said and turned back.

'Thirteen blocks are not many...we can go to each one and ask,' I calculated.

Anushka looked at me, 'That's more than two hundred houses. Wait, I know someone in my building. Her name is Dhuni. Her father is in the accounts section in Delhi University. I know how to liquidate her. And if she can't help then we'll come here and ask everyone. Don't worry.'

'To liquidate her...?' I asked.

'Everything is fair in love and war. Let's go,' she said. Dry petals of the rose once again received dew drops but its veins were still dry. If wishes are strong, the world walks with you.

We decided to go to her apartment. The only difficulty was to deal with her father because he was strict as she told me.

We reached her place and entered her dining room. It was a Sunday. Though her father was busy with small flowerpots in the balcony; his old, frightening eyes were watching every move of ours when we entered. Then he turned back, his glasses mostly hiding his face. Slowly, he walked to the other room and I greeted him. When I glanced back, he smiled at me. His smile reeked of wickedness, and something inside me told me he held many secrets within him. His black eyes kept watching us and moved to the other room. We talked and aunty served us tea in bone china cups. After some time, her dad entered wearing a new t-shirt. 'He must have changed into that without taking a bath,' I thought.

'So what's going on, children?' he asked and sat on the sofa. Aunty gave him a cup of tea. Anushka put her cup on the table and explained, 'I'm from Delhi and he's from Mumbai, and we both work for a multinational IT company.'

'Oh IT, how much do they pay?' The question was actually weird and we looked at each other.

'They pay enough for survival,' I replied with happiness. She pinched me as I replied in the same tone in which he had asked the question. She hit me on my toe.

'It's okay till you guys are young; try and join any government service.'

'But they are all corrupt,' swinging my legs sitting on the sofa, I laughed out loud. Dhuni looked at me angrily. I realized what I had said wasn't any less than a crime. I kept silent. He didn't respond to the answer, finished the last sip and put the cup on the table and left.

'You children enjoy, I'll make something for you to eat,' aunty also left.

'Why do all professors always behave like horrible philosophers?' I thought. The thread of my thoughts broke when I heard some funny comments from Anushka: 'In the age of Android, your dad is seriously the Windows 98 types. Less features, not compatible to modern apps and you can't play a fast game otherwise there will be a system error,' she started laughing.

'Shut up, he's my dad. Stop it,' Dhuni made her stop. She

looked at my shoes. I pushed back my dirty shoes coated in mud.

Now only the three of us were in the room. Anushka told Dhuni, 'Your dad works in Delhi University, so ask him if he can provide some information about Pakhi.'

'You know my father...' Dhuni looked at her.

'Yes, I know...Windows 98.' Anushka laughed.

'There is nothing called confidentiality in India. If he wants, he can provide us with the details,' I thought for a moment and gulped some bad words for him.

'It would be better if you ask him directly; he can tell you what to do.' If your own father is strict, you can manage but handling somebody else's strict father can be quite a challenge. And then suddenly I realized, when my dad shouted at me there was only person who could handle him—my mother. I knew how to charm my way into a lady's heart. I went to the kitchen and asked aunty if I could speak to her. She responded turning to me, 'Yes, what happened?'

'I want to talk you about something important.'

'Yes, sure, tell me, you're like my son,' she washed her hands in the basin, and wiped them with the towel from the hanger.

'Come,' we walked to the sofa in the hall. We sat there and I told her everything without being emotional and the reason for our visit. She heard me out and asked just this one question, 'It's been more than two years; do you still love her?'

'Two years aren't enough to forget someone, it will take at least a lifetime and who knows about the next life, so just need a little help to find her.' With a smile on her face, she put her hand on my head and said, 'Wahe guru will help you. Wait, I'll talk to your uncle and he'll help however he can. She went into the balcony and talked to him.

'Call him,' I could hear only these words. I came to the dining room and sat on the sofa.

'You could have spoken to me directly, there was no need

for aunty to intercede.' We all sat together and then discussed everything.

'It's not easy, you will have to put in some labour,' uncle said and put on his big broad eyeglasses. 'I will,' I answered.

'Come to my office on Saturday. This Saturday is a second Saturday so it will be a holiday for most of the staff members. There won't be many people and it will be easier to search from amongst old files. However, there are thousands of files you will have to look through. That is the only way to find her address,' he took a piece of paper, wrote his number and gave it to me saying, 'call me once you reach office.'

'Thanks a lot.'

'No problem. Say thanks when you get the address. I'll help you, but don't discuss it with anyone because these are confidential files.'

'Sure, uncle.' I breathed in a sigh of relief. Dhuni and Anushka were shocked seeing the way he treated me. Then we all had lunch together.

As soon as we left her home, my cell phone rang, and I was called to office the next day because there was some code deployment. I had to reach there. Dhuni's father had said the right thing that IT sucks. I still had three days before Saturday, so I left Delhi in the night and planned to come back on Friday night... and then something happened...

Unfolding Truths—Inbox (786)

'Why didn't you tell me that you were going to meet my bhabhi,' Vishal kicked me.

'You were sleeping when I left,' I replied, I had a cup of coffee in my left hand and held a piece of bread in my mouth.

'You asshole,' he kicked again on my back...quite hard this time.

'Stop it. Now I have to send these reports.'

'Baby, it's 8.00 p.m.'

'Yes, I know, but I have to go to Delhi this Friday so I have so send these. Now don't disturb me for two hours,' I said, turning back to my laptop.

'Yes, yes, do your work, else Neha will feel bad.' He tried to pull my leg.

'It's official not personal. By the way, Neha is married and she is your manager, too,' I smiled at him.

'Fuck off, man. I've seen those party photographs in which it looked like she was completely all over you...,' he said.

'That was a group photograph and she was standing just behind me not "falling all over" me...' I laughed. He stood up and said, 'I'm worried about you. The *India Today* survey says 12 per cent people are in open marriages where partners know and are okay with affairs outside marriage.'

'Don't worry, I'm not going anywhere. Why don't I have three hands? I have to send these reports as soon as possible,' I took the piece of bread in my hand and said, stretching my body.

'You have three hands. You are using two and there is one between your legs that you haven't used for very long.' He showed me a paper making a hole in that and wrote ass just above it—asshole. He laughed devilishly and I showed him a vampire face. He ran away to the hall.

I sent those reports and a pop up message flashed on my Google talk. He was Vivek, my new office colleague. He was famous as macho man among us because of his machogiri.

Vivek: What's going on, man? She was looking so gorgeous and hot today.

Me: Who?

Vivek: Deepika... Look at her curves 34-25-36 and especially her ass...perfect.

Me: Lol. Why do you do all these things?

I wanted to know why he was always this weird and he had a simple answer for that.

Vivek: Girls always like my herogiri. I'll not die with the regret that I couldn't sleep with the sexiest girl. I will not die thinking that I drove only Maruti 800 in today's world of Ferrari, Ascari and McLaren. Even you should try once.

Me: I'm happy with my Bajaj Chetak life.

I had some other priorities in life and I believed that even girls who like boys like this, liked them only for thrills and sex; in reality, they don't really 'like' them as people. Girls like funny people to have fun with and want a decent man to spend the rest of their life—my mind said this and my heart supported it and I accepted this fact wholeheartedly.

Me: Chal...logging out. Take care. Good night.

I checked my G-mail account, clicked on sent items randomly and looked at Pakhi's photographs and went through the longest voicemail to listen to her voice. Even small things associated with the one you love give you great pleasure.

I had been doing this for more than two years now. Sometimes

I used to think, 'Am I okay? Why am I doing the same thing every day? Is this not madness?'

At the next moment, I assured myself that if this was madness then I was happy with it, at least I didn't need sleeping pills anymore like I had for the last six months. I clicked one of those old chats.

Chat with Pakhi:

Pakhi<m...16cool@gmail.com> to me

10:46 p.m. Me: What are you doing?

Pakhi: Nothing, I have been waiting for you for the last 45 minutes.

10:46 Me: Oh my shona, I'm so sorry. I was with Mamma.

Pakhi: What is she doing?

Me: Packing food and the basen ke laddoo I got her to make especially for you.

Pakhi: Oh really, say love you to aunty. And what time will you reach here?

Me: I'll say thanks to mom and keep love you for me. I'll leave in the night and will reach there by 7.00 a.m.

So what's the plan for tomorrow?

Pakhi: We'll go for a movie. What should I wear?

10:48 p.m. Me: Why? You don't have anything to wear?

Pakhi: I'm confused.

typing...

Me: Whatever you wear, it will suit you. Well, you were looking very good in blue and white salwar kurti the other day.

Pakhi: Thanks

10:49 p.m. Me: For what? :O

Pakhi: For being with me always. I love you.

Me: Love you too. Now go to sleep. It's late. I'll wake you up when I reach.

Pakhi: No

Me: What no?

Pakhi: Just want to hear your voice for some time.

Me: Okay, you come in your room. I'll call you.

Pakhi: Luvvvvvv youuuuuu

Me: Love you tooooo.

My cell phone beeped with Anushka's message. I checked and saw that I already had three missed calls from her.

Had she found her address? I thought and called her back immediately. She didn't pick my call and that made me nervous. I started calling her incessantly and then I called on her landline.

'Why are you not picking my call? What happened? Did you get her address?' I shot several questions at her within seconds.

'Calm down…calm down. My phone was on charge in my room. I called you thrice earlier.'

'What happened?' I was desperate to know.

'I got a call from Dhuni that her dad has shortlisted some files and hopes he will be able to help you. You come on Friday, we'll find some solution,' she said.

'Mom is calling, talk to you later.' She disconnected the call.

My eyes fell on my inbox. It showed…Inbox (786)

As Rahim Chacha said that 786 is a lucky number and coincidentally my inbox showed 786 messages, so I was curious to open it. I just clicked on it. The mail had come from the email id—m…16cool@gmail.com. Everything stopped for a moment and I started going through it—

```
Hi Anuj,

I know this will come as a shock for you and
that's obvious. Please read this mail patiently.
  We realize many things in life when we lose
everything. I don't know at what stage I am but
I loved you a lot and this heart still beats for
you. I have made many mistakes but there were some
reasons behind them. I don't know whether you love
```

me still but I want to share a few things about my life that I never shared with you earlier—

Every girl needs a support. Every girl wants love of a family. Every girl wants to be happy and loved by someone in her life. My dad was everything for me. I could leave anything in my life but never my dad.

My mom and brother sent me to my Mama's place in Delhi for further studies when my dad had a paralysis attack. I was in tenth standard at that time. I never wanted to leave my home. When I came to Delhi, I used to cry and missed my dad a lot.

A mother is her daughter's best friend. She understands and guides her during her teenage especially when hormonal changes occur in her body because she has also gone through the same phase.

A girl really needs a mother and I didn't have her in my life after leaving my home. There was no one to care for me, to discuss about my days and my problems. First time when I had my periods, I cried in fear and then my Mami took care of me. Many times, I folded a cotton cloth and used as a pad during my periods because I felt embarrassed and shy to discuss. I used to cry alone regretting being a girl. I was so alone. It was very difficult for me to live alone but I had no other option. When I went home during vacations, I had a different world with my family but when I came back, it was difficult to manage. I was a girl who really needed parents.

My friends felt so proud when they got good marks but even after scoring the highest marks, I couldn't feel that happiness because when I was back from my school, my Mamma and dad weren't there to celebrate. If I called then they congratulated me but that wasn't enough.

When a girl says that she wants 'space', that doesn't mean distance. It means she wants an open sky to shape her desires, wishes and dreams. Many times, I felt insecure because I had no goals and then my best friends—Neha and Deep—helped and treated me like their younger sister. They made me an extrovert and then I started making new friends.

I had completed my twelfth standard when I met Ajay. We were classmates at the medical coaching institute. We were preparing for CPMT exams. We became very good friends. I discussed about Ajay with Neha and Deep. They were happy. Days passed happily in this wonderful amity and I didn't realize when we fell in love. He was so loving and caring. Whatever a girl needs and whatever I missed in my life, he completed everything. Now I had someone to discuss and to share my feelings and problems with. I started loving him like anything. I came very close to him. Sometimes we had a physical relationship because we didn't have any secrets between us and he wanted to love me with no boundaries.

I loved him so much that I never gave it a second thought and accepted him completely.

However, life has its own way. After six months, he started hurting me. Whenever I tried to talk, he started fighting with me. One day he called me and said that he couldn't be with me because he never saw any future with me. I felt cheap and broken.

When he left me, my life came to a standstill. I

had some serious health problem. I had my friends Deep and Neha who supported me at every point of time.

Even though I used to call Ajay waking up in the middle of the night but he used to fight and hurt me. One day he changed his number and left me forever.

Neha opted for medical studies at Bharatiya Vidyapeeth, Mumbai; and Deep joined a Biotech course in Manipal University, Karnataka and I opted to study Life Sciences in Hansraj College, Delhi University. I was alone but anyhow I managed my life as I had understood that life was cruel.

After all vicissitudes, I never believed in love and relationships because I was deeply hurt.

When I came out of all this, you came in my life and we became good friends. I had never even dreamt of this true and pure friendship. We hadn't seen each other for eleven months but I didn't feel that you were not with me even for a single moment. Any girl dreams for a guy like you and I started loving you but I didn't want to break my friendship and somewhere I also feared that someday you'd also leave me, so I never told you that I love you.

You always pampered me as my dad used to, you listened to me as an elder sister and you always discussed everything with me like the best partner in the world.

When we met first time in Delhi after eleven months and you kissed and proposed to me in the theatre, I had accepted you as my love and everything but I still had fear. We loved each other deeply but I fought with you many times in frustration because I needed you physically close to me and that desperation came out as anger. Being physical doesn't mean you have to have sex every time but that you need a physical presence to support, pamper and love you. When a girl loves someone, she wants to come close to her love emotionally and physically. Physical need is equally important as emotions and feelings in a relationship. Moreover, when you came, we had a good time. Months passed and you fulfilled all my dreams.

Misunderstandings come in every relationship and I fought with you many times. I was wrong at many points of time but I didn't mean to hurt you. Day by day things went in the wrong direction. I tried to manage but I couldn't. Expecting too much in a relationship brings trouble sometimes and I did the same. However, when I thought to meet you, next day you were with me. I just loved the way you made me feel every moment. I can surely say it's impossible to find a guy like you.

It was summer of 2010 when after watching the fifty-first movie in the theatre, I got a call from Mamma that dad was in the hospital and we were without clothes in a bed. You told me to go after sometime, as it was too hot outside. We went physical and intimate and when I left, I had lost my dad. I started hating love because I was very hurt. I had lost everything after losing my dad.

We didn't talk much during those days and I stopped talking to everyone. I stopped bathing and eating. I just missed my dad sitting in my room and cried. I used to throw the food in the dustbin and one day when Mami came to know about it, she realized that I had some serious problems.

My menstruation cycle stopped all of a sudden for three months. I was shocked, took the pregnancy test, and told my mother. When my Mamma and mami talked to the doctor, she said that mental stress can temporarily alter the functioning of the hypothalamus—an area of your brain that controls the hormones that regulate your menstrual cycle.

I used to fight with everyone and I started hating people who talked about me. For two months I didn't go to college and when you called me, I needed you and wanted to tell you everything but I shouted on you and we couldn't manage.

We fought and I cried alone. The mishap happened so I couldn't meet you.

After two months, I started going to college and if someone listened to me, it was Arpan—but he was just a friend then. He cared for me and listened to me. He never made me feel lonely. He was a very good friend. Many times, I felt you in his deeds and behaviour. I started sharing my feelings with him and he started liking me. I never liked him more than a friend.

One day he called me for a movie, I went with him, as he was my good friend but nothing more than that. In the middle of the movie, he kissed me. I tried to stop him but that happened and he went ahead and came physically close to me.

After returning from the theatre, I didn't talk to him but I missed you too much. Whenever we fought and cried in frustration, he made me happy. Even in college he took care of me when my dad left.

I started talking to him and again we went for a movie and the same things happened. I regretted after doing this but I failed in front of hormonal changes in my body. I started hiding things from you but I never loved him. I didn't know what I was doing. This continued for a few fortnights.

One day, our group of friends planned a party at his place. He called me to his house an hour earlier, however. When I reached there, no one else had arrived yet and he asked me to wait while he made coffee for me.

I was having coffee and he hugged me from behind. I tried to stop him but he forced me to come closer. By hook or crook, his wishes won and what happened next was something I never expected, not even in my worst nightmares. He pushed me on the bed and put on a condom. He started tearing my clothes off while I struggled under him. I screamed and when he came to know that I had my periods, he slapped me and threw me on the floor. All this felt like a horrible dream. I ran away and cried the whole night.

That day I tried your number but your number didn't exist because you had moved to Mumbai. Before I could try to find you, next morning Arpan felt sorry for whatever he had done but it didn't matter anymore. I had lost my virginity. That was a day when again I was hurt and felt cursed being a girl. Without saying anything, I ran away.

Again, I thought of contacting you but I had already hurt you a lot and it had been more than two years. Why would you accept me; someone who had lost her virginity with someone else. Making myself believe that you must have forgotten me, I never tried again to contact you. I used to cry alone in my room. One day when I fainted in college, my friend Shruti asked about me, and I told everything to her. Shruti called my mother and Mami. They took me to the doctor to consult about my health because I had lost seven kgs in a month. It was shocking for everyone that I was suffering from Hemolytic anaemia. Red blood cells in my body were getting destroyed and I had a lower than normal number of red blood cells. My condition worsened and I needed blood every fortnight.

One moment I was happy and the other, I shouted. I only started thinking about myself and became desperate to get whatever I wanted to achieve. People started discussing about me saying things like I was insane and mentally tortured. I wanted to prove to them that I was still a girl, who was the prettiest of all. This thought gave me some comfort and my life became normal. I never regretted whatever I did. My arrogant behaviour hurt many of my friends. I could see changes in my language and behaviour; I was becoming very selfish and spent my day indulging in daydreams. My mental health worsened even more. Mamaji and Mamma consulted doctors; they diagnosed me as a patient of Narcissistic Personality Disorder (NPD), Psychotic and Manic disorders together. This was horrible to accept.

They suggested consulting specialists for these disorders. I had never heard of these disorders and then I read about them and that scared me. Everything was ruined in two weeks. Every day seemed like the last day of my life and every week that I lived was a blessing. Doctors said that NPD and psychotic disorders were severe and I couldn't be cured completely. I started living my life on mercy. Everybody treated me like a patient and that made me weaker every day. Everybody started ignoring me; I lost my friends and their trust because I used the wrong way to achieve my goals. I was scared of nights and sleep. In the middle of the night, I used to wake up and cry. I stopped going to college. It took me around six months to come out of this horrible phase of my life and these disorders but I was still having the mood swings. Things changed and I started going to college and completed my MBA.

Yesterday, I was coming back from my office and my eyes fell on an unknown girl who was reading a book. Firstly, I ignored her but the last name written on the book caught my attention as the first name was hidden by her fingers. I went ahead and asked her about the book. When I turned the page, it was you. I couldn't understand what was that and what to do. I took her number and borrowed the book. I just finished the book in half an hour.

Anuj, I know I have hurt you but I love you a lot. I know it's not possible for any guy to accept a girl like me but I know about my guy:) This heart still beats for you. If I still deserve you, I'll wait for you till the last breath.

Waiting for your call. I'm coming to Mumbai next week, hope to meet you.

Your still-stupid girl,
Pakhi.

Who Could Wait for Heaven?

My eyes were wet as I sank to the floor. There was pain in them but those teardrops poured a deep happiness into my heart. I hugged the laptop and closed my eyes for some time. *Why? Why? Why did you take so long to tell me?*

I could feel her presence in my veins. That moment was untold, unpredictable and not less than a dream that had come true. I felt a tingling in my stomach and anticipation that I couldn't explain to anyone. I felt captivated, charmed, ecstatic, elated and joyous... all at the same time. My lips stretched into a broad smile and my eyes filled with tears of patience, love and dedication.

Those pages stayed in my life forever. For a moment I couldn't understand what had happened—I had found the one for whom I had left everything, my friends, my family and my life. All my dreams came to life once again. In my madness of love, I took my cell phone and dialled her number and then suddenly our old days came in front of me. It was tough but I disconnected the call and at the same time, I called Anushka. Those rings seemed much longer than the other day. I was walking in the room, smiling alone with tears.

'Again you've called me in the middle of the night. Do one thing, come marry me and be with me forever. Can't you see me happy?' she said in an unclear voice.

Her tinkling voice made me laugh but I couldn't because I remembered and realized something. I followed her words and responded, 'Anushka, I'm serious. I wanted to tell you something from so many days but didn't have the courage to say it. We both are very good friends, we know about each and everything. Even I know that you're thinking the same thing now.' She fell silent.

'I was just looking at my mail and I got her back in my life,' I said in a very low voice. Suddenly she asked, 'What did you say?' I replied in the same tone, slow and low, 'I just got her mail. She's coming to Mumbai next week.'

She started shouting, 'You bitch...bastard...fuck off...you got her back. I'm so happy for you. Tell me everything from the starting, how and when?'

'She has sent me a long mail. I knew that she loved me a lot and she has written everything in it and has given her number so that I can contact her. I don't know how to react.'

'Then what are you doing? You have her back...the one you waited for so long. I salute your love story, man. You won't believe in the morning my left eye was flickering and now I know the reason why,' she seemed emotional but happy for me.

There are some beliefs about flickering eyes in Hindu mythology. Some people believe it brings good luck and some believe it brings bad luck. If a man's right eye flickers, it's a good sign for him and if his left eye flickers, then it is considered bad. In case of women, it's the opposite.

'This should be a great meeting, so I'm coming to Delhi tomorrow. You sleep, see you,' I said.

'Good night. I haven't seen a crazy guy like you. Inform me whenever you reach here, meet her and meet me if you get time from your so called shona,' she teased me but there was sweetness, love and care in her words. She disconnected the call. I threw the phone on the bed and walked to the kitchen and had a glass of water, moved to the wash room and washed my sleepy face.

I booked a flight ticket for 5.00 a.m. as she used to leave for her college at 9.00 a.m. so that was perfect time to give her a surprise. I texted Meera early in the morning—This may surprise you but the day has come to meet my girl. I'm leaving for Delhi, boarding the flight, so switching off my cell phone. Thank you for being with me, my dream has come true today.

'What will I gift her, I don't have anything to give her! If I don't get anything in the morning in Delhi, then…' I felt helpless, as I had nothing to gift her. I looked at the statue of Lord Shiva and smiled with pleasure. I picked the red sacred thread and kept it in a box. In Hindu religion, marriageable maidens pray to Lord Shiva for the husband of their choice. They even fast on Mondays to push their wish list to Lord Shiva. According to Hindu beliefs, the month of Saawan, which begins mid-July, is auspicious for unmarried girls and if they observe somwari vrat (fast) on either one, two or sixteen Mondays, they are blessed with good husbands.

Therefore, I picked up the thread as a sacrament of Lord Shiva. I came downstairs. 'Should I call an autorickshaw?' Manoj, the security guard asked. He always took care of me and I used to sit with him whenever I felt alone and we shared a strong bond. He used to discuss his problems with me.

'No, I'll catch one from the next crossing. I'm leaving for Delhi, you take care of yourself. I discussed about your salary with the manager of the society, hope you'll get it this week.' I patted his shoulder and picked up my bag.

'Thank you,' he looked happy.

I caught the cab at the next turn after walking for five minutes. My heart began racing the moment the cab pulled into the airport parking lot.

I could sense the excitement of passengers waiting to be flown to their far-flung dream destinations like me.

'Lover Boy,' my mind said to me in a honeyed voice. This happened after almost two years when my mind and my heart felt the same thing at the same time, 'Lover Boy' else my mind always talked about pros and cons, and my heart always talked about love.

I reached the airport. There were different kinds of people

there. The smell of sweet perfume mingled with the smell of jet fuel. I recognized the smell of fading perfumes that women were wearing. The whir of wheels on marble and concrete mixed with the mechanical, yet pleasant, voices on the public address systems calling for someone to go to the nearest courtesy phone, or announcing that flight 346 is now boarding at gate 7. As I joined the queue at the check-in desk, I could see groups of people talking about travel and what they would do when they arrived in Delhi. They seemed excited. Their faces were brimming with happiness. I developed a virtual relationship with the passengers who were travelling to Delhi; it soon seemed like I knew every one of them.

There was still an hour to go before I reached my destination. I felt the thrum of the engines at take-off and the vibration of the plane during the flight in my skin and I could feel the fragrance of love all around. I closed my eyes and smiled alone.

'What happened?' A cute baby girl sitting next to me with her mother pinched my hand softly, raised her eyebrows in naughtiness, and blinked. I smiled at her. He mother held her hand and said, 'Baby, sit properly.' I touched her cheeks softly and asked, 'What's your name?'

Before her mother could say something, the baby girl answered, 'My name is Mukta but Mamma calls me Mukku beta.'

'Hawww shoo shweettt...'

She looked so cute and her babbling voice won my heart. As I heard a couple behind me chatting about the weather in Delhi, it looked as I expected...so romantic. Things become pink, days become long, and nights become short when you fall in love. Life can change anytime, so just live the day and consider it the best day of your life.

Knotting threads of romance in my heart, I was on the way to meet her.

The sky seemed dark when you were sad,
Morning became bright when you were glad,
Your laughter changed the mood of thousands of people.
The world needs you to be happy,
Your smile made my life forever...
My love doesn't demand to meet you every day,
My love doesn't demand to talk to you every moment,
I just love you every night in my dreams,
And that is enough to make my day.
My love needs to be with you forever...
I won't promise to build a castle in the desert for you,
But I can give a kiss on your forehead every morning,
You made me the winner of this world,
But I'd love to be a loser in love with you.

And the plane landed at the Delhi airport...

A Melting Sunrise with Her

$\mathcal{I}$ caught the airport express from the IGI airport to New Delhi Metro station. I dialled the number she had mentioned in the mail. One…two…three…four rings later the call was picked.

What to say? I felt nervous. 'No need to feel nervous. You know her,' I motivated myself.

She picked my call, 'Hello.'

I didn't reply because this was the time to have fun.

'Hello. Who is this?' she asked again.

'May I talk to Pakhi?' I just said this, though I knew she was on the call.

'Anuj!' the voice came from the other end. I didn't speak a word in response and remained silent. She repeated my name again and I responded in my style as I used to—

Tu door hai aur pass bhi, teri kami hai aur ehsaas bhi,
Jeena chahta hun har lamha tere liye, tu zindgi hai aur ek aas bhi.
Chadar ki andheri silwaton me teri yaadon ko gale se lagaya,
Juda na tha kabhi ek pal tujhse, tujhko hamesha apne kareeb paya,
Yun toh log bahut the is rah par sath dene ke liye,
Apne apne hote hain, yeh tujhse milke is dil ko samajah aaya.
Tere aane ke jashn me yeh dil tujhko salam karta hai
Parwah nahi ek pal ke liye jab yeh zamana tere naam se badnaam karta hai
Chal un gamon ki silwaton ko mita, ab ek naya jahan banayein,
Jahan bas hum sang jiyein,
Aur sang hi ek doosre ki baahon me hamesha ke liye so jayein.

Words were coming from my heart itself and then I felt the magic of love. Love never demands preparation, it just happens and demands purity of heart, which makes everything special and precious.

Sniffing over the phone, she cried with my lines and said after sometime, 'Is this is a dream? Where are you?'

All of a sudden I felt like a boy who had lost his mother in a crowded fair and after crying in the middle of the fair alone, he finds his mother.

'Your voice has changed and you've become mature it seems,' I said softly, in a romantic voice.

'Where are you?' she asked again in excitement.

'Just next to you,' I said.

She took a minute; it seemed like she raised her neck to find me and said, 'Please tell me. Where are you?'

'Just near you,' I was standing at the same place we had first met at CP. She was looking here and there, standing not far away from me. I disconnected the call and tried to approach her.

'This is called destiny and the world is round, hence proved.' My heart said and mind passed a green signal to it. Dreams come true if you are dedicated to them.

My cell phone vibrated, I took her call, 'Where are you?' she asked.

'At the same place where we met the first time,' taking the support of the escalator railing, I replied.

'Oh really,' she murmured into my ears from the back. She turned to me and my eyes saw an oval face, curved eyelashes, and her emerald hazel eyes glistening in the bright sunlight. Her hair was dark brown, almost to the point of being black and it hung loosely over her shoulders giving perfect contrast to her dress. She looked prettier than angels when her untied hair fell on her cheeks with a light gust of wind that came from somewhere. Black fish shaped earrings suited her fair complexion. Light chocolate colour lip-gloss on her pink lips seemed like rose petals. She was wearing a grey coloured t-shirt, earphones in her ears, red cheeks, and cute face as ever. We stared at each other for a moment and then she jumped on me.

She just hugged me tightly and I took her in my arms. People were looking at us but that wasn't the day to think about others, that was the day to love. We just hugged each other for a couple of minutes, 'I missed you a lot.' She sniffed two three times. 'I missed you too,' and then we let go.

My eyes were also watery because those dreams were in front of me.

'You haven't changed a bit,' I just blushed.

'Yes, same as I was, except these marks on my hand,' she showed black spots of syringes on the upper side of her palm. 'Now these will go away soon,' I said and she agreed with a smile.

'But you have changed a lot and that was important by the way. From those weird shoes to your hairstyle, everything,' she grinned.

When she touched my hand with hers, I forgot all my worries, tension, and tiredness and felt that someone is there to listen to me with love and care.

She looked like old wine, prettier and enough to make my heart skip a beat. 'Someone else is roaming around in your mind or are you still thinking about me?' she laughed and pointed to the exit of the metro station.

'No, just a girl is roaming around in my mind who is the prettiest one I've ever met.'

'Now this is not the time to listen to old instrumental songs, it's the time to rock on my beats. Let's go home,' she said in her own style.

'But what shall I do there?' I tried to say something but she interrupted and said, 'Why? Why can't you go with me? They aren't aliens, you shouldn't have any problem meeting them,' she pulled my hand. She walked and I just followed.

What was going to happen at home—that was the only question in my mind at that moment.

Mission In-Laws

I had met her mother at her cousin's wedding but this was the first time when I was officially invited to their place. I was happy but nervous. Meeting someone from future in-laws' family is tougher than clearing IIT with a few months of preparation. My mother didn't know this would happen, so she hadn't prepared me for this.

Two white marble pillars leading to the entrance, a large wooden double door, pointed at the top and antique silver knockers on the door. The long garden view around the walkway leading to the entrance with many small flowerpots looked beautiful. I looked at the nameplate on the door.

'What happened? I've never seen you like this before. Are you okay?' Standing at the door, Pakhi asked. She rang the doorbell and my heart started beating wildly.

'Hey, stop,' I pulled her hand. I rearranged my shirt, set my hair like a kid and took a long breath. I smiled at her.

'Anuj, she's my mother, not your boss. No need for formalities,' she rang the bell. I started memorizing our values, culture and tradition. I was gulping air and her cousin opened the door and looked at us. 'Hey, how are you?' she asked both of us.

I nodded with a reply, 'Good.'

'Come, come,' she said loudly and called her Chachaji. First thing that I knew was, one should keep away from males at the in-laws' home, as they will try to pull your legs and ask weird questions. In Indian families, the toughest part is to make the father, elder brothers and other elders happy. Therefore, I prepared myself to smile at silly jokes and to agree to whatever crap they would say. We entered and I just followed Pakhi. My situation was like a school child on the first day of school who just followed his teacher's instructions.

'Be cool and just chill,' she smiled, blushed and looked happy but I looked nervous. 'A-N-U-J-J-J-J...' she looked at me and held my hand when nobody was watching. Her home looked like a palace as it was built with mostly white marble and granite, with grand balconies and circular staircases. The fragrances of roses and lavender filled the air. There were small lamps glowing on the window in a row, few around the sofa and one on the table with a sunrise couple in a dancing pose. There were old brass showpieces hanging on the front wall. I liked the deer neck with long horns. A honeyed tone of ankle bells and bangles dropped into my ears and I was alert like a puppy. Her mom came to the hall.

∽

'Mom, this is Anuj,' she said to her mother. Pakhi pointed her hand first to me and then to her mother in respect, 'Anuj, my mom...'

'We have met before and know each other,' she smiled. I came forward and touched her feet, 'Namaste, aunty.'

Pakhi grinned and blinked at me when I touched her mom's feet. The first card worked, I felt happy. Long way to go, I thought.

'How are you, beta?' she asked me. She was wearing a blue sari with a golden border. The way she talked made me conscious for a moment that she wasn't like other mothers.

'I'm good, aunty. She has told me many things about you,' I replied.

I wanted to say Ma as she was going to be my mother-in-law but I stopped myself.

'No stupidity...no stupidity,' I remembered.

'Even I've heard a lot about you,' she gave me a smile. I was confused whether it was a good or a bad thing. 'Sit comfortably,' her mother said, wiping her forehead with the towel in her hand. I was sitting on the sofa next to Pakhi. 'She must be cooking something for me,' I guessed and then realized, 'she didn't even know that you are coming...popat.'

'Take it easy, it's not easy to become a son-in-law in a few minutes, you haven't impressed her yet. What's next in your love quiver?'

'So, would you like some coffee?' aunty asked. 'So would you like to have coffee or juice?' Aunty repeated again and broke my reverie.

'No, nothing, aunty, I'm good, will have after sometime. Can I have a glass of water?' I smiled and responded very politely. I didn't talk to my own mother like this. Everything was fine and I was comfortable now. Mother-in-laws are not that bad. They are bad only in Ekta Kapoor's serials.

Pakhi blew a kiss in the air to tease me and fortunately, aunty didn't notice that. I made a sad face.

'You've come home for the first time, you have to have something,' aunty left for the kitchen. Making myself comfortable, I looked around. Two walls of the room painted with white paint and other two, with light blue that matched her sari. A lamp with a heart shaped bulb was glowing at the corner of the room. Pakhi jumped in my sofa, kissed on my cheeks unexpectedly, and said in a low voice, 'You impressed my mom, carry on.' I pushed her, 'Hey! Someone will come and will kill me. Please...'

'Muahh...love you,' she blinked her eyes and sat on the other side of the sofa.

I looked at the photo frame with the picture of her father on the table with a mala of flowers on that. Her Vijay Mama and Geeta Mamiji entered. Her Mamaji was in a white kurta and Mamiji in a black sari. She looked so gorgeous. All of them looked as if they were going to some party. A long gold chain around her neck and big round earrings gave me a rough idea of their bank statements. Then, I corrected myself, 'They are going to be a part of your family soon.' I stood up and touched their feet.

'I can't talk much as I have a throat infection,' he said in a butter-soft voice.' I didn't know what to say to that so I gave a smile saying, 'No problem, really nice to meet you.' Her Mami started questioning me about Mumbai and celebrities. We laughed and enjoyed.

'My mami has performed plays at the Prithvi theatre in Mumbai during her college days,' Pakhi came to her and hugged her.

'Oh, that's nice. So where did you study from?' I asked because Pakhi's mother was busy cooking for me and her Mamaji was reading the newspaper sitting on the divan in a royal style. 'I did my graduation from Ramjas College, Delhi University and completed my MTech from IIT, Mumbai.'

Pakhi added, 'She used to do modelling in her college days, is it right Mamiji?' She smiled, 'Yes, but after my marriage, his family didn't allow me to do these things and I left,' she said looking at Mamaji.

'Then come to Mumbai,' I said.

'Yes, next week mami is coming with Mamma and me,' Pakhi said.

'I'm not sure, beta. I won't get leave from office,' her Mami was working with a bank.

After sometime, her Mamaji left, and we all sat together. I won their hearts without any blunders.

After spending almost half a day at her home, in the evening, we all went to a mall. The whole day we enjoyed together and the day actually made me feel that I was with my mother-in-law. Now it was time to leave but we planned to go for a movie the next day.

After shopping with her and her Mamiji, I planned to leave.

'I will take a cab from CP and call me, once you reach,' I said to Pakhi who was standing in front of Shri Gol Gappe corner at CP.

'What's going on? Who is going where?' her Mamiji asked

turning towards me while having the last bite and wiping her mouth with a handkerchief.

'May I leave?' I asked while taking out my wallet to pay the guy

'Stop it, don't be ridiculous,' she stopped me and paid herself.

She added, 'You can leave, if we allow you to. It's already eight. Let's go home and you can leave tomorrow morning,' her Mamiji said and Pakhi looked happy.

'But…'

'No buts no ifs, dinner is ready at home, just come with me.'

'Is it fine to stay at her home? What will others think?' I was confused and they forced me to stay. Then I decided to leave after dinner. We reached home and her Mamaji opened the door.

Love of a Mother-in-Law

Sitting around the dining table with her mother, younger brother who just came when we reached, and Mamaji was enough to make me nervous. However, I didn't have cold feet and doubts about my decision; if they asked me to marry Pakhi, I was prepared to say a happy yes but this wasn't going to happen as I had thought. It was uncomfortable for me sitting in front of them and just being the centre of attention.

'Doctors say we should eat properly and without any obligation. *Why aren't they concentrating on their plate instead of looking at you?'* my mind asked.

Because I'm the scapegoat, I thought and passed a fake smile to her Mamaji.

'Feeling nervous about eating around people is common among men, women, and children. Social notions tell us that it is not nice to be seen eating in public, mostly for fear that people will think we're eating too much, and will look fat or undesirable,' my mind said, I re-worded inside again and coughed noisily when I meant to smile.

'What happened, beta?' her mother asked me, pouring some water in my glass.

'No nothing, I'm fine, just have a cold,' I said. I was sitting just in front of her mother, to my left was Mamaji and to my right was my love...my precious...Pakhi. I didn't want to look at my left side because as I had heard and had seen in my family, Mamas always poke their nose in others' business. From Kans mama to

Shakuni mama they all had to butt in in others' lives. Before I could conclude anything, 'So, what do you do in Mumbai?' he asked me.

'It seems he's still hungry,' I thought. I turned at him and answered, 'I work with an MNC as a software engineer and deal with clients.'

One more question came from the other side, her brother asked, 'So what's your annual package?'

'What the hell, he's asking about my salary?' I wanted to kick on his ass but a *saala* is always *saala*. I added few more thousands to my actual salary and said, 'It's around seven.'

'Not bad,' her Mamiji appreciated, the rest just smiled and her brother looked at me with a square face as if I had said something wrong.

'Let him eat peacefully,' her mother said, looking at him. Pakhi kissed me in the air and that was a signal for me to relax...it happens in Indian families. I looked at the wall clock and it seemed hundreds of years old. The clock said 9.45 p.m. Aunty placed a big bowl of kadhi in front of me.

'Enough, enough, aunty,' I said.

She placed two more chapattis in my plate. It's really tough to be a son-in-law. I finished as fast as I could, as that dining table seemed the stage of drama...the Indian melodrama. She ladled one more spoon of kadhi in my bowl and two big spoons of rice in my plate, 'No aunty, I don't want any more,' I smiled at her and burped

'Excuse me,' I said.

'Just a spoon of rice, you're not a kid, just have it,' her mother said. However, I said no but I dreamt for that day and prayed this would continue in future.

'How is the kadhi, beta?' aunty asked me.

'Yes, it's good. It's tasty. You cook like my mother,' I nodded with respect. 'Pakhi made this. Very rarely does the sun rises in the west,' her mother said. Pakhi looked happy because I liked the food. Licking my finger, I looked at her, 'You cook well.'

Her Mamaji put a laddoo in my plate, 'One won't make you fat. Moreover, girls care about their figure, not boys. Have it,' he said. All of us stood up and washed our hands. It was late now and I had to leave for home. 'Hey where is my cell phone, I have to leave,' I asked Pakhi.

'Just a minute.'

'It's too late, stay here, you can leave tomorrow morning,' aunty said.

'No, it's only 10.00 p.m., I'll go,' I said.

'Shut up...I'll drop you early morning,' Pakhi said, looking for her mother's approval.

'Don't threaten him. Is this a way to talk?' her mother said, 'Beta, it's too late, take rest and don't worry. Tomorrow Pakhi will drop you at Kashmiri Gate or Dilshad Garden early in the morning,' her mother tried to convince me.

'Is it fine to stay at her home? Where will I sleep if I stay?' I thought. This was not a part of my plan.

'Don't worry; it's just like your home.' We came in the dining hall and I sat on the sofa. Her mother came to me and said, 'It's quite late. I wanted to talk to you about you and Pakhi. Next week we're coming to Mumbai, then I'll talk about it.'

I guessed that she was talking about the seven vows.

'My family is also coming to Mumbai. Then we can talk.' I informed her.

'That's great news, beta. I'll talk to your mother. God bless you.' She put her hand on my head and looked emotional.

'All mothers are like that.' I hugged her partially.

'Pakhi, show him your room and keep the AC low and one water bottle on the table, if he needs it. Good night, beta. See you in the morning and sleep well.'

'Come,' Pakhi said. Her mother went into the kitchen and we went upstairs.

Mangal Sutra and the Message in the Wallet

'You are lucky to stay here at my home. Boys rarely get the opportunity to stay at their in-laws' home before marriage,' Pakhi unlocked the door, pushed it open and switched on the lights. The room had a sweet coffee fragrance. The walls were painted in light, warm colours like cocoa, pink, beige and white. A coffee table with some armchairs stood at the corner of the room with a couch next to it. A big cute teddy bear soft toy was kept on the stool next to the window and a framed collage of her college photographs hung just above the wooden bed. There were a couple of beautiful lead crystals on each of the two bedside tables with artwork on the walls. Her room looked so serene, it just screamed romantic and relaxing.

Once I had heard my neighbour, Sharma aunty, talking to mom about her son-in-law never staying at her home and how she appreciated his values and respect for his in-laws. I remembered those words now.

'Pakhi, staying here for the whole night doesn't seem like a good idea,' I said, even though I wanted to stay with her forever. However, sometimes you have to compromise with your wishes and consider your social values.

'Mamma knows about us, so there's nothing to worry about. And, anyway, it's only for one night; I'll drop you home tomorrow morning,' she said as she lit a few small red glass candles. Moving to the door, she closed it smoothly and silently.

'Still, I'm not comfortable here. What will your Mamaji think? The way he was asking questions has made me really hate him.'

She laughed aloud.

'Don't laugh.'

'It's okay. I'll drop you early in the morning. Now sleep, and if you need anything, call me,' she said, straightening the bedsheet and pillow and keeping the water bottle on the table.

'Hmm...by the way your room looks so romantic and beautiful,' I said admiringly, looking around once more. A few chocolates, wrapped in heart-shaped boxes were kept on the table. She picked one up and gave it to me. 'What are you thinking?'

'Just imagining how sweet those moments will be when I drop you to work early in the morning.'

'Now sleep,' she urged.

I untied my wristwatch, threw my wallet on the bed.

'Hey, is that my card?' she said, suddenly spotting a card in the wallet. She grabbed it. Happiness shone on her face like a child, and her tears didn't take long to spring to her eyes.

'It's still in your wallet...and with the gift wrapper that I wrote on, too! I can't believe it. And it's been more than two years since I gave it to you.'

I came close to her and wiped her tears. 'And you know you tore it up when you saw this in my wallet and I fought with you when you did.'

She smiled tearfully, 'I remember you shouted like a mad person.' She touched that card and those two pieces of paper on which she had written two years ago: 'Time may be good or bad but I'm always with you.'

I hugged her from the back and kissed her on the neck. I held that card and wrapper tight while locking her in my arms. We didn't say anything for the next few seconds and then she looked up into my eyes. Words failed us but we said everything there was to say the moment our lips touched. We kissed tenderly and enjoyed the moment. She bit me lightly on my neck and left a mark there. Biting my ear, she murmured, 'I love you. Good night.'

'Hey stay here for some time,' I said.

'Mamma is waiting.'

'Okay, just one minute,' I unzipped my bag and took the box from it and said, 'I have got something for you.'

'What's that?' she asked very eagerly. As usual, she felt great and looked cheerful.

'Just close your eyes. This is for you.' She closed her eyes and I came ahead. I opened the box, picked that sacred red thread that I had kept in the box while leavening from Mumbai. Her eyes were still closed and I tied it around her neck. She touched it and then opened her eyes, looking at it. 'I couldn't buy anything for you, so keep it as a mangal sutra.' We looked into each other's eyes.

'It's enough to make me happy and when you are with me, I don't even need anything.' Her eyes sprinkled with tears and happiness. 'Now you close your eyes. Even I have something for you,' she said.

'Oh, really!'

'Yes.'

'Close your eyes,' she said.

I did as she said. She tied something around my neck, 'Don't open your eyes.' It felt like a metal chain.

'Now you can open your eyes.' I opened my eyes. It was a gold chain.

We hugged each other. 'I love you a lot but please keep it with yourself,' I said.

'Shut up and no bakwas, keep it and if I see you without it then you're dead.'

'But this is not right. It's too costly and I can't take it. I'll take it the next time I am here but not this time please.' I tried to make her understand that I couldn't take that.

'Anuj, what right or wrong. Things we've done so far were not always right,' she blinked her eyes, 'Don't worry and you look good in that and treat it as my bridle which will keep you on the right track whenever you go astray.'

She laughed and continued, 'Now I'm going. See you tomorrow at the breakfast table.'

'You are going without giving me a kiss,' I looked at her like a baby boy.

'Of course not, my horse,' she laughed again. She kissed on my cheeks and moved to my lips. We smooched for a long time. 'Good night,' she murmured. 'Bye.'

'No...' our lips were rubbing against each other still.

'Mamma is waiting downstairs. Leave me...hmm.'

'I want to love you.'

'Not now. I have to go now but some other day.' She released herself and moved out of the door, looking at me wildly.

'I love youuuu...bye.'

I lay on the bed and relaxed a bit. I had to leave tomorrow morning. I looked outside the window and fell asleep thinking about our future. I looked at myself again in the mirror, and that gold chain became a part of this new life.

I never unhooked it after the day she hooked it around my neck.

Rapid Rules to Impress the In-Laws

Though I was lying on the bed, I couldn't sleep.

Couldn't we meet tonight? *I want to meet her. I'm bored here.* I thought and closed my eyes. I was thinking about all the conversations again. After closing my eyes, I felt how beautiful life was. I could feel that happiness in my heart but genuine questions came in my mind about meeting my in-laws.

Did I look fine in front of her mother? Did I eat properly in front of her Mamaji? Did he see me when I blinked my eyes and kissed her in the air? Was I a blabbermouth, a gasbag? Or was I an introvert, shy and meek? How did her mother feel about my arrival?

These thoughts were jolting my mind. I was smiling remembering all the conversations once again, closing my eyes.

I recollected all those conversation that Sharma aunty had with my mother during her daughter's marriage. I loved to sit with aunties and learnt many rare things but I never thought that sitting with Sharma aunty would really help me one day.

She gave the best eleven RRII (Rapid Rules to Impress In-laws, I named it R2-I2) for the final innings at the in-laws home ground:

1. Do your homework. Before going into your future in-laws' house, be sure you know a little bit about them. Talk to your partner, and ask them about their parents so that you can get to know them better. This way, when you meet them, you can talk to them more, and bond with them with ease.

2. Don't forget that they may have the same insecurities about you that you have of them. Maybe they want you to like

them, but they just don't know how to do it. Just accept the situation and be yourself, be relaxed, and encourage them to be themselves. Remember that your spouse comes from this house, there has to be a common thread somewhere for you to get along.

3. When meeting the mother of your better half, it's all about the compliments and smiles. Make sure that you compliment the legendary mom. There is nothing better or impressive than giving your future mother-in-law a compliment. All this shows your care and is a sign of respect for her and for her family.

4. Ask about her health before you take care of yourself. Take interest in your in-laws' life and their extended family. Be ready to help and ready to serve and then she'll come to know that you will make her princess happy for life. This is a great way to get to know more about them.

5. Join in the family fun. If you're meeting your future in-laws, then it means that you're going to be a part of the family soon, so don't be afraid to join in. You can be friendly with the family, so give your lovely smile and don't alienate yourself.

6. Respect their objects no matters living or non-living. This is the rule of respect and then they'll respect you in return.

7. Make your own identity and be genuine in front of the family. It's not easy to impress your in-laws, especially mother-in-law, but you have to do so with your positive attitude and respect for her. Being nervous is obvious but don't pretend that you're too open. Be decent but don't flatter.

8. Bring a symbol of respect; it can be in form of sweets or gifts. When you don't know about their choices, it's better to bring sweets or chocolates for kids in the family. Alternatively, if you're visiting them for the first time then bring a flower bouquet. Moreover, in some cultures, decent gifts or a token of shagun in the form of money seems the best symbol of respect for the whole family.

9. Dress for the occasion. Show class, yet be a bit formal. Unless you're meeting the parents over a picnic, dress up a little. That's not a very serious thing to remember but you can't ignore it. Look decent because your mother-in-law's eyes are always on you.

10. Talk to the family, as you're a part of it but don't get too involved. A healthy conversation is incredibly necessary when it comes to the first meeting because the whole family wants to see what you're all about. Don't be afraid to impress them and this is the time when you should show them who you are, and what about you made your better half fall in love with you.

11. Don't feel shy or uncomfortable talking to your better half while you're meeting your in-laws. Don't forget that you're there for your better half so give time to everyone. This way the family can see why your presence is important for your better half.

I was happy and I followed each rule as well as I could. They were happy, too, I knew. God bless you, Sharma aunty.

A small blue bulb was glowing just above the aquarium in the room and soft light was falling beautifully on those colourful fishes. My silence was broken when a small blue fish hit the glass wall. I blinked my eyes and smiled.

I couldn't sleep in this completely new place, though I had already made many plans to spend nights here with my better half.

Holding the pillow in my arms, I was smiling for no reason, and then I heard a knock at the door. I ignored it and slept again lazy as I was.

Some Sparks in the Dark

My cell phone beeped after some time. With half closed eyes, I shoved my hand under the pillow and looked at the screen... *Pakhi calling.* Rolling in my bed to the other side, I picked her call, 'Hey, what happened. You're still awake?'

'Open the door, I'm standing here in front of your room,' she murmured over the phone. I pushed the blanket to the other side forcefully and stood up to open the door.

'What happened at this time?' I was scared that something had gone wrong. I opened the door, she was standing there in her nightdress, looking beautiful in the moonlight.

'I have been knocking at the door for so long, how do you sleep?' she said as she entered.

'Like the prime minister of our country without any worries,' I said, still sleepy-eyed.

'Very funny.' She removed her stole and fixed her hair, threw the phone on the bed and locked the room.

'Hey what are you doing, what if someone finds you here,' I was scared because if someone caught me, my impression as an innocent guy would go down the gutter.

'Everyone is sleeping, no one will come at this time,' she came to the aquarium and touched the glass wall with her small fingers.

'How's my room?' asked she.

'Nice room, romantic enough but have you come here in the middle of the night to ask me this question?'

I moved ahead to her book rack from the other side of the

room, 'Nice collection.'

'And you know, I grew up with my friends Friday, Saturday and Sunday,' she said pointing to the aquarium.

I laughed, 'Why Friday, Saturday and Sunday?' Her long hair reaching down to her waist and purple nightdress with a black border made my heart race. I saw her first time in the dress that I imagined her wearing after our marriage but God had some other plans for us and that night seemed made for me specially.

'Because I spend the entire day with them on Friday, Saturday and Sunday, so...' she smiled, touched them with her small finger again and then turned to me. 'Oh you have my book, *Journey of Two Hearts*,' I rose as if a baby finds her mother after a long time and took it from the shelf.

She blushed.

The room was bathed in blue light and she looked like a fairy under the blue moon with whom I was going to spend the rest of my life. My mind said, 'Go ahead and kiss her. Should I tell you every time?'

'I know, I'm young enough, there is no need to tell me. I want to kiss her but from where to start and how to do that,' I replied to my mind.

'Oh really, you're not doing this for the first time. Go ahead bastard, she's your life partner and you're going to spend the rest of your life with her,' my mind gave a strong punch that I deserved.

A pretty girl walked towards me and seemed in a romantic mood to do something mischievous when she locked the door. 'She locked the door not to kiss you...' I understood before my mind could say few more words. It's a very awkward moment when you know each other and you both are alone in a room but nobody starts the final over and who is going to be bowled out tonight, you never know.

I was curious to know about her skills. She walked up to me with a beautiful smile, and without speaking a word; she pulled me to the corner of the room. My heart started beating wildly. Those feelings made me feel like I was meeting her for the first time...Love is just like that, fresh and alive.

However, nothing happened. She showed me very beautiful handmade cards on which there were small radium coated stars glowing in dark with these words—Times may be good or bad but I'm always with you.

'How's this?' she looked at me, a piece of diamond in her earrings in blue light looked so beautiful and twinkled. 'So beautiful, just like your twinkling earrings,' I touched her earrings with my fingers softly. She shivered when my thumb touched her neck. We hugged each other tightly and she winked at me.

'You are beautiful, you're so sweet,' I said. She looked so gorgeous in the blue light and more beautiful with every passing moment. I saved those moments in my eyes forever. I saved them in my heart to tell our kids about how I met their mother. 'I'm lucky and I love her so much,' I said to myself and was lost in heaven.

'Okay,' she pushed me back and approached the corner of the room next to the sliding window and the table where there were few cosmetics like lip-gloss, eyeliner and few of her pictures sticking just above the table on the wall. She stood on her toe, raised her neck to open the cupboard, which was just above those cute pictures of her.

Before she could do any magical acting, I went there and took out the coffee maker from the cupboard. She turned to face me. Now she was in between the table and me. She pulled my waist to her stomach. I put the coffee maker on the table. 'Thanks,' she laughed and pushed me to the other side.

'Let me make coffee for you,' she blushed and prepared a cup of coffee within minutes. She took a sip to taste it and put it on the table next to the bed. I held her with a stroke and pulled her towards me. Now one of her hands was in my hand, my other hand on her waist and her other cold pleasant hand on my shoulder. I started swirling round and round holding her. She laughed, 'What are you doing?' 'Stop it...Stop it.' Still laughing, 'You know salsa?' I smiled again.

'Not much.'

'I'm not as good as you are,' she took one round holding my first finger.

This time she held me more professionally and repeated the steps that we did. I synchronized with her after a few steps and for the next few minutes, we danced for the first time together. 'I love you,' she said, dancing on the floor with love and happiness. I came close to her. 'Are you trying to kiss me?' asked she, showing her earrings. For some moments, I didn't move from my place. I just felt something cold, wet and a pleasant touch. She kissed on my neck and then looked into my eyes. I did the same. There was love in them and I was ready to lose my senses and be hypnotized for the whole night under the same roof. Once again, I felt love was blind when she held my hands tightly, closed her eyes, opened her lips and started breathing fast.

'Should I kiss her?' I thought. 'You are an asshole...' my mind repeated. It's better to walk, if you can't run rather than doing nothing.

So I didn't listen to anything, just followed my innocent heart. I came close to her cheeks and felt her warmth. It's very rare but you spend some of the sweetest moment with your partner just before marriage, because one brings all the dreams in his/her eyes and the other steals all those dreams and makes them true.

You don't need huge amount of money to be happy and to live a sweet and romantic life, you just keep fulfilling those very small expectations that your love expects from you.

'How sweet that moment is...' I thought. She remained silent but her lips were shaking and my ears could feel those pleasant sounds of her breath. That time I was ready to refuse heaven for my angel under the roof.

Love never demands anything impossible; it demands your trust and belief, your love and care and respect.

I couldn't control my feelings.

∽

Her fragrance overruled my senses and I touched her pink lips with my thumb softly. My fingers were behind her neck and thumb on her chin. I looked at her beautiful face in the blue light, kissed on her forehead and then bit low...bit low...and bit low. Unexpectedly she placed her hand on my lips saying, 'No. Not now, you have to wait for a few months, can't you?' we were looking into each other's eyes without blinking. 'I can wait for my whole life for you but is it necessary?' I placed my hands on her cheeks, kissed on it, smiled and hugged her. Those arms were enough to spend the rest of my whole life, I didn't need anything. 'Oh! So innocent you are,' she murmured and blew a gust of air into my ear. She tilted her head slightly, pressed her lips on mine and closed her eyes. Those dry lips were not dry anymore. She lost her senses as I had already. I went ahead and removed her lip gloss with my tongue, tasting it. She nibbled on my neck lightly.

'I love you,' she murmured, ran her hands in my hair and then tightly wrapped me in her arms.

'I love you too,' I continued. We forgot all about where we were. We were lost...lost in love.

I looked at her once again. She was looking pretty; I pinched on her nose. She took a last sip of coffee and kept the mug on the dressing table. We were hugging each other and she picked the coffee mug from the table, looked into my eyes deeply and asked, taking a sip, 'Do you want a sip?'

'Yes, I do,' we came close once again.

She suddenly pushed me on the bed and kissed with a sip of coffee.

She touched her lips to mine very hardly and during this warm kiss, she gave a sip of coffee from her mouth and transferred almost the full sip. I took a full sip, gulped, and licked her lips. That was the nectar of my life. Coffee on her lips, coffee on my lips, I enjoyed this coffee smooch.

I was smiling looking at her, imagining my days after marriage. We didn't stop and allowed ourselves to get lost in each other. That was the moment when we were two bodies but one soul. She looked at me full of love and expectations in her eyes. 'Next time, we'll try with chocolate paste,' I murmured into her ear.

'Shut up,' she lightly kissed on my lips and asked, 'will everything be fine?'

'I'm always with you,' I promised her, holding her hands tightly.

Even after two years, nothing changed the passion, the dedication and the love that filled colours in every moment of our lives. Patience makes your wishes stronger. I wasn't less than a winner of the world because I had my love now. I was happy but it had taken more than two years which had shown me all colours and shades of life. 'You're not alone now,' I assured her, touching her cheeks. In those romantic moments, a few teardrops came out from her eyes. 'Hey! What happened to you...my love?' I touched her cheeks. She looked into my eyes like a baby girl. Those were the drops of our feelings which became stronger over a long period. 'Nothing,' she said. I kissed on those teardrops one by one and took all her pain in between my lips. Love isn't all about being with each other all the time, it's all about how you make someone feel that he or she don't need heaven when you are with them. 'You're so bad,' she said in mock anger. I pulled her chin up and asked, 'Why?' 'You are,' she wiped her tears and hugged me tightly. I let her be like that. 'I'm always with you. I apologize for my mistakes,' she held me as tight as she could. 'I'm not going to run anywhere, you can release me a bit,' I murmured into her ears.

'Shut up...'

We felt each other, fell into bed and our breath connected us.

A Cup of Coffee under the Sky

'Let's go upstairs,' she said, putting her chin on my chest and looking, somewhere in the room. Her soft cheeks felt like feathers on my chest and her hand was still running over my body. Her hands were pleasantly cold and I felt a deep happiness inside that I had never imagined before. In these two years, she had grown up and become mature. 'You want to go upstairs in the middle of the night?' I asked her, placing my hand on her cheek. She put her chin on my chest and looked at me. 'Yes, in the middle of the night. I want to see the stars. We won't get this chance again, so let's go.' She kissed my chest.

'But first wear something warm, it's too cold outside.'

'Of course, I'm not going out in my underwear.' She wore her nightdress and set her hair. Her voice was like a baby's, her eyes that of a naughty girl and her caring nature—my heart and mind agreed, *She hasn't changed.*

She took a cup of coffee in her hand and with silent steps, we came outside the room. I looked around downstairs and she locked the room expertly without any noise. 'Hey, slowly,' I murmured. She pulled my hand and we went to the terrace. I walked to the other side of the terrace.

'Hey, don't walk here and there, just come and sit.' She called me. There was a small shelter in the corner of the terrace, where she used to sit in the evenings. She placed a mat there. We sat leaning on the wall. It was a full moon night and a few stars were peeking out from behind the clouds. The icy air danced across my skin and left goosebumps in its path. She moved, slid to my side and sat in front of me. I hugged her from behind, sitting comfortably; we didn't speak. We were looking at the stars which were playing behind the dark clouds.

Clouds can form virtually any shape, and sometimes you see your own desires in them. *What are my desires?* I thought. I hugged her tightly and got the answer—*to be with her forever.*

'Do you know when we die, we go up there and become stars?'

'Oh! Is it? Then we'll be shining stars,' I put my chin on her shoulder.

'Where is my dad?' she asked without any pain in her voice, holding the coffee mug in both her hands. She always missed her father; he was the only one who had fulfilled her every wish without any questions.

A father is the one who looks out for the entire family. A father is his daughter's best friend, who understands her and tells her the difference between trustworthy and fake relationships. Seeing his little girl grow up is tough for every father but the best father is the one who comes forward and talks to his daughter openly about everything like a friend. From putting the baby to sleep, changing her diapers and giving her baths to shaping her self-esteem, self-image and confidence, he always walks with his daughter.

'He is not there; he's just here in our hearts.' I took her hand, put it on my chest and then kissed it. We sat there for more than an hour and talked about our future because we had promised not to discuss our past.

'Hey, let's go, it's been more than an hour,' she raised the coffee mug up to my lips and I gulped down some coffee.

'Yes, else I'll lose my perfect son-in-law image in front of my mother-in-law.' We stood up. She covered herself with her stole. We came downstairs without making any noise. While opening the door, I saw her cousin coming up.

'Now I'm gone,' I pinched her. She looked around. 'What are

you doing here in the night?' Pakhi asked her cousin and unlocked the door.

'Di, it's not night, it's 4.30 in the morning,' she smiled with a naughty expression.

'By the way, if it's night then what are *you* doing here?' she blinked and her question made me embarrassed.

'Nothing, go to sleep,' she replied.

'All the best,' she teased her and turned back to go downstairs.

A Warm Night with Extra Dots

We entered the room. She was shivering. 'I need a coffee,' she said, rubbing her hands. I walked up to her and pulled her to the bed, murmuring, 'Yeah, I need this coffee lipstick too.'

'Shut up. I'm shivering.' I covered her with my arms and legs. I was lying on top of her and her lips were only a few centimetres away from mine.

'Leave me.'

'No...'

'Let me go. Someone will come.'

'No...'

'Please...'

'No...'

She gave in and we kissed. We closed our eyes, lost in our own world. Now she was on top of me. We kissed for a long time. She ran her hands over my well-formed pectorals. She held my nipples, kissed them, pressed them between her thumb and index finger and gently caressed them. I put my arms around her and held her tightly. She placed her head against my chest. It felt like heaven. She looked up and I bent down and kissed her. When we stopped for breath, she gently pulled her face towards my nipples. 'Why don't you suck it for me,' I said. We had never done this before but whatever was happening was giving us pleasure. Bodies which had been living without love for so long were actually experiencing real moments of passion and love.

'I have never done that before,' she replied, kissing my lips once again.

She took one nipple between her lips. She licked it at first and then started to suck on it.

'The things that you are supposed to do, she's doing, asshole...' I thought again but ignored it as I felt good.

'I want to melt in you,' she said. I held her with one arm and with the other I took hold of one of her boobs and started to squeeze it. She tried to push my hand away gently but then she let me fondle it. She was quite excited by the sucking.

I placed my palm on her right hand. I grabbed her breast. She looked up and smiled at me. It seemed this was going to be the most interesting day of our life. I felt like a groom on his honeymoon night! *Is this our first honeymoon?* The same stupid question and the same stupid answer came to my mind...yes, our honeymoon before marriage.

We were quite excited now. I wanted to feel her body. She looked hotter than I could ever imagine. I held her hand and pushed her into bed. I touched her fish-shaped earrings, the same ones I had gifted her on Valentine's Day and then softly touched her neck. She was looking at the ceiling and I was looking at her. We both were lying in bed.

'What are you doing?' she looked at me and whispered. She placed her index finger on my lips and said, 'I just want to love you.'

She swept her hand over my hair and kissed my forehead. I was out of control now. I grabbed courage and gently put my whole palm a little up to feel the softness of her body and closed my eyes.

'Anuj! I'll kill you,' she murmured in my ears. She held my hand tightly when my hands were moving up to the neck from the stomach. I rolled over and covered her body with mine. I just held both her hands and came close to her face. I sensed her warmth. I kissed her on her lips deeply and she responded with the same passion. I licked her lower lip multiple times. 'Hey, pull the curtains and then come close to me,' she whispered. The next moment I closed the curtains and came to bed.

I smiled and responded by claiming her lips in a passionate kiss. I pushed her back but then, suddenly, she locked my lower lip with hers. She didn't just love, she owned me. I wanted to hold this moment forever. She turned and lay on me and kissed my chest, neck, shoulder and almost every part of my body but a few areas were still untouched because I was still in shorts. I rolled again and placed both my palms on her waist and then later one moved to her breast. I just caressed her breast with my right hand and she hugged me tightly. I started kissing her neck and shoulder. While moving to her shorts, she gripped my hand hard and pushed it inside her shorts to open it.

'Don't you wear underwear?' I murmured.

'I'll kill you. Nobody wears them at night. I'm going, bye.' She felt shy and tried to release herself.

I pulled her back and hugged her in the bed. I could feel the softness of her body and the pleasure it gave me made me feel like I was in heaven. She synchronized with me and we started kissing each other madly once again.

I placed one palm on her breast and the other moved her T-shirt up to the neck. She was in a black and white bra but that was enough to make our moments colourful.

'You are beautiful,' I whispered into her ear. She pulled my face up. We smooched with passion and energy. She tried to remove my T-shirt while we were kissing madly. I removed it myself, and she jumped on me. We were exploring each other's mouth for a minute. Then, I removed her T-shirt too and threw it somewhere.

I turned her and worked my way down, dragging her shorts down. 'What are you doing?' she said.

'I just want to love you more than I ever did.' I snatched her shorts off. Why don't garment companies use better buttons and zips? It never works at the right time. I couldn't open it easily but she paddled her legs and threw the shorts perfectly.

I kissed her cold stomach and went lower. She gripped my chin and pulled me to her breast.

'Just love me,' she said. I held both her hands and kissed her shoulders, neck, went lower and licked. She closed her eyes and said, 'I love you.'

I kissed her breast. 'I missed you a lot in these two years.'

She ran her hand on my back, in my hair. 'Then fulfil all your desires tonight,' she grinned at me.

'You're looking so pretty and awesome.' I lay down and she just sat on my tummy, and bent down to kiss me. She then climbed down, unfastened my shorts, and pushed them down. She went lower while I looked at the ceiling and closed my eyes. I was lost in her love and she was in mine. I could feel it growing in size with each move. I could see that it was obviously pleasing her. It was fascinating. It was a nice feeling. I leaned forward and grabbed her shoulder and pushed her a bit lower. I gently squeezed them. She bit my tummy.

'Ahh...' I felt like a current had passed through my body. She was still laughing. Suddenly I put my hand on her stomach, and then went lower. She kept silent, tried to stop me but my hand moved as deep as it could. I touched her pubic hair, opened her legs in excitement and let out a feeble moan.

She pulled me into her arms and legs tightly. It was quite exciting and gave me a pleasant tingly feeling.

No clothes on our bodies, rubbing against each other, we were lost...lost in love. I could see she was beginning to get excited every minute. 'I love you,' she said. Her chin was on my stomach, and her eyes were seductive. 'Did you feel good?' she asked softly.

'Yes...' Before I could say something else, she went lower and kissed my thighs and around. The next moment was not less than any heaven.

By this time, I could feel how hard I was. She was in ecstasy and just pushed my head closer to her crotch. 'Just love me.' I grabbed her in my arms more firmly. Our eyes were partially closed when she took something from under the pillow and gave it to me. A packet of condoms. 'Hmm,' she murmured.

'Is it the right time?'

'I don't know. I want to be yours forever.'

'But...'

'No buts...let's do it.' She tore the packet. I just held that and touched the vulva. Before I could go ahead, someone knocked on door. 'Hey, someone is at the door,' I heard some noise and then a few more knocks.

She covered herself with the bedsheet and sat up. The voice at the door was her cousin's. When I looked outside the window, it was almost morning.

She stood up. 'Shit, I'm dead today.'

She put on her clothes and took a few sips of water. I was still naked and quickly pulled my under garments and T-shirt from under the bedsheet, found my shorts on the other side. I pushed the curtains to the end. Her cheeks were red. She stood in front of the dressing table and set her hair with both hands. She looked at me and asked, 'What happened?'

'Thanks for coming back into my life,' I smiled.

'You are mad. I'm gone today. See you at the breakfast table. Get ready,' she said and left. She went downstairs. The clock said 6.04 a.m. I heard aunty ask her where she had been. I thought for a moment: *Now both of us are dead.*

∞

After sleeping for an hour, we all gathered at the breakfast table. I was still sleepy and thought, *Doesn't she know about yesterday?*

'Good morning Anuj,' Geeta Mami wished me, dragged the chair back and joined us for breakfast. Her brother had left for office and that made me feel comfortable because the way he was asking questions yesterday made me feel like kicking his ass. Nevertheless, her Vijay Mama was sitting just in front of me. I wished everyone and sat down.

'So did you sleep comfortably last night?' her cousin asked, looking at me and then at Pakhi.

'Yes, I was tired, so got up late this morning,' I replied.

'What are your office timings?' he asked, taking a plate. Her mother said, 'Let's stop this interview session and have breakfast.' I answered him, as he was elder to me, so ignoring his question was not a good idea. Also, he was going to be my relative in the future and Mamaji plays a big role in marriages and functions, so I smiled and answered, 'Nine to six.'

Her mother put one big wonder pot of poha on the table. She took a wooden spoon, served the poha, poured orange juice in glasses and placed a few slices of toasted bread on the other plate.

'Do you want salsa or jam or sauce?' Geeta Mami asked, passing bottles of sauce and homemade jam.

'I'll take jam,' her cousin said.

'So how many brothers and sisters do you have?' Mamaji asked, spreading butter on toasted bread.

'I have one elder sister and she's a lecturer in an engineering college. My dad works with BSNL as the chief accounts officer and mom takes care of our properties and lands.' I gave him the full introduction, so for the next question he'd take some time.

'Good, all working people,' Mamaji said. I nodded.

'So do you have any interest in business?' he asked and stood up from the table.

'As of now, I haven't decided because after college I got a job in Mumbai and it took up all my time but I won't continue this forever, so let's see...' I finished the last sip of juice. My watch said 10.30 a.m. and I had to leave. I washed my hands and checked my cell phone.

'Hey, I have to leave,' I said to Pakhi. She called her mother and said, 'Mamma, I'm going to Bangla Sahib Gurdwara and will drop him at the metro station,' she took the keys of the car.

I touched the feet of Geeta Mami, Vijay Mama and aunty. Aunty packed something for lunch, gave it to me and said, 'We will come to Mumbai next week and your family is also coming, so let's meet there. Take care and call her when you reach.'

Pakhi drove to the Gurdwara Bangla Sahib which is a prominent gurdwara in Delhi, known for its association with the eighth Sikh Guru, Guru Har Kishan. The pond inside its complex, known as the sarovar, whose water is considered holy by Sikhs and is known as amrit.

We removed our shoes at the entrance and washed our hands. While entering the gurdwara, we covered our heads. She took her stole on her head and I tied my handkerchief. She looked like a newly married bride. Sitting on our knees, we prayed for some time. 'What did you wish for?' I turned to her. She looked at me and we stood up. Pushing her stole behind her ears, she replied, 'Those are secrets, we shouldn't discuss them.'

'But the one you wished for is in front of you.'

'I'll kill you. Let's go now.' After receiving halwa as prasad, we moved towards the exit.

'Don't you think we should have pani-puri before leaving? If you don't want to, it's okay. I'll manage...' I said, pointing at the pani-puri wala.

'How dare you have that without me,' she walked up and we had pani-puri.

She drove me to CP metro station and before opening the doors we had a long kiss inside. 'I love you,' she murmured.

'Love you too. Will wait for you next week, take care. I don't want to go but your mother will kick me out,' I kissed her on her forehead.

She laughed.

At the Beach in the Rain

'Hey it's 6 o'clock in the morning. Get up,' I was still dreaming when Pakhi called me early in the morning. The last fifteen minutes of sleep in the morning is like nectar in heaven but it seemed that the hands of the clock were running a race. I could see a pinkish light glow in the room when I turned in my bed and looked out of the window. The sun was preparing to shine brighter and I wanted to sleep for a few more minutes. 'No, get up, please,' she poked me again as her sweet voice fell into my ears. I opened my eyes. Dots of sunshine dancing across my room through the curtains and the aroma of honeysuckle was making its way through the open window from the vine outside. I could hear the movements of newspaper guy outside. The birds twittering, sunlight streaming through the green leaves and the smell of rain from the night before made me feel better.

'Why do we wake up so early?' I stretched my body as much as I could.

'Because I'm coming to meet you,' she said tremulously.

'Can't you come right now? I want a tight hug,' I opened the window, looked at those hills, and felt the fresh, cold breeze.

'What time you will reach?' I asked.

'I've reached Bombay Central. I've come with Geeta Mami, Mamma and Nanu. See you at Juhu beach at 11.00. Get up and don't be late.'

'Okay,' This wasn't the first time she was coming to Mumbai but this was the first time we were meeting in Mumbai. I was really excited to meet her and reached Juhu an hour before I was supposed to. I had just crossed the road when it started raining. I ran towards a shelter. I called her, 'Hey where are you?'

'Just reaching, you know how the Mumbai locals are...just ten more minutes,' she said. As the sun follows foggy weather, she came following the rain. The waves of the sea and the marching clouds started to play hide and seek with us, clouds thundered and went away in a while.

∽

Raindrops shuck into her dimples and a few remained on her eyelashes. She looked more beautiful when she tucked her wet hair behind her ears.

'What are you staring at?' she waved her hand in front of my eyes.

'Nothing, just wondering if this is a dream.' We started walking along the sea.

'It's not a dream, it's raining and you're looking good,' she grinned and we stopped. Rains had made everything romantic and looking into each other's eyes, we kissed. Droplets of waters sprinkled on our bodies and we forgot the world. We cherished those moment in the rain. We were almost lost in our world, standing along the sea with rain pouring more love into our lives.

She locked her small fingers with mine and I looked into her seductive eyes, 'Love you,' she said.

Eyes say many things when they look at you. She got her reply from my eyes. We walked along the waves that touched our feet. Raindrops on her face looked like dew drops. I just wanted to touch them, feel them, taste them. We enjoyed coconut water and boiled corncob in the rain.

'Hey let's go,' I held her hand.

'Where?' she asked, surprised.

After spending such a pleasurable time with each other, we

were both deeply happy.

'Let's go to Bandstand and sit there,' I said.

By the time I finished saying that, she had already stopped an autorickshaw and we headed towards Bandstand. Sitting in the rickshaw, she asked, 'So how many times you have come here and with how many girls?'

'I can't remember the numbers exactly but yes, with many, and many times. I love this place.' I was serious and my words seemed true. She just smiled and said, 'Hmmm' and nothing else. I looked at her, touching her hand with mine, 'What happened?'

'Nothing, I just feel bad for those girls,' she broke into a laugh.

'Hey!' I laughed too. I was reminded of all those memories and conversations. I was walking with her after two years. I just saluted God and said thanks from my heart that I'm still alive, still in love and still with her. We walked a few steps and reached the CCD at Bandstand.

'Let's sit there,' I pointed to CCD. She nodded. We took the front table from where we could see those waves,. She picked the menu card.

Suddenly she asked, 'So you didn't miss me?'

I just turned my eyes to the other side, as I never wanted to hear this question, as I never wanted to remember a few things and I never wanted to answer this. She looked into my eyes for a while. 'Tell me,' she asked again with curiosity and expecting to get a romantic reply from me.

'Pakhi, I was so busy in these two years, I didn't get a chance to remember those things. I was busy with my work, so nothing else came to my mind,' I replied but that most beautiful face looked sad now. Those pink lips looked yellow and she looked at me with her beautiful eyes pleading. 'Yes, you've become a big person,' she smiled and ordered one Mochachillo and then she read something to ignore me.

'Seriously...you didn't miss me?' She was still stuck at what I had said to tease her.

This time she looked so emotional, so cute and as innocent as she looked first time when we met.

'I am happy that you lived a good life in these two years. Nevertheless, you don't know how much I cried for you, how much I missed you and every moment that we spent together. You forgot everything,' she almost cried.

A waiter came and put a glass of coffee on the table. I didn't say anything. I let her say everything that she wanted to because two years were not a short time, so there were many things to share. She added, sniffing as though she had a cold, 'Every day before going to sleep I used to read the seven cards you made for me and then I slept with those. One day early morning, when Mamma asked me about those cards, I told her about you. I hugged her and cried a lot. First she shouted at me but she understood me when I told her everything. I just wore the same earrings that you gifted me on Valentine's Day because you said I look good wearing those earrings.

'My favourite dress was the one you gifted me on our first Valentine's Day. Everything that was related to you was the most precious thing for me and that helped me remember you but couldn't reduce my pain. I know it was stupid but I learnt this stupidity from you and you didn't miss me,' she was sad and her eyes were wet now. She turned her face to the other side. She didn't look at me, she was looking at the adjacent table now. I could only see her hair. I smiled and didn't want to share the moments that I had faced in her absence. *Pain is not to be shared if you truly love someone, spread love that makes the relationship stronger*, I thought.

I touched her chin with my right hand and held her hand with the other. She forced herself not to look at me, then I held her hand with both my hands.

I picked up the heart-shaped card, put that on the table and pushed it in front of eyes that were still staring somewhere else.

She looked at that pink handmade heart-shaped card and then looked at me. She picked it up. It said:

You always make me feel that I don't need anybody,
Since the day I talked to you.

I held her one hand in mine and said, 'Every night I missed you and every night I just tried to know why I'm here because you were not with me that time.'

I put the second card on the table, very softly and with all the love. She took it and that said:

I love to wake you up early in the morning because your voice makes
my day and your laugh, fills happiness in my life, and when I talk
to you, I forget everything.

She looked at me and continued, 'Every night I slept with my tears. Each and every moment was hard to live and your absence made me helpless.'

I brought out the third card and it said:

After talking to you for so long,
I again wait for the next moment to talk to you
What is that, I don't know but something special I feel.
When I call you again and again, you shout, but I miss you. . .
But I love the way you shout and then care for me, I just love that.
And yes…your smile after a big fight, I lose my heart all over again…
I don't know what magic it is but I love this.

I didn't say anything this time and just picked up the fourth one and put that on the table and few drops of tears dropped on the table. The fourth one said:

Many times, we fought, many times we shouted,
but after that always you made me cry because I missed you a lot,
I am sorry but don't fight but talk to me,
I miss you a lot, when you don't talk.

Teardrops were continuously wetting the table and this time a drop of tear dropped on the fifth card, which said:

I just love to pamper you, care for you but I feel bad when you cry alone.

The fifth card made her eyes more wet, she kissed on that teardrop which dropped on the card, 'You are still mad,' she wiped her tears too.

'I don't want to say anything.' I put the sixth card in front of her and the sixth said:

You are the best girl I've even seen, whenever we talked over the phone, there is always a thought in my mind that I love you so much…

'If you think, you should go for the seventh card, which is not as simple as the other ones, I hope you'll accept from your heart whatever I've written in that. Should I give it to you?'

I gave a sweet smile and she deserved it. I was waiting for her reply.

Surprisingly, she checked her bag, 'From where did you get these cards??' Still lost in her bag, running hands in it. I smiled but didn't speak.

'Anuj, tell me. Did you take all these from my room that day?'

'No.' I said.

'Don't lie. I had all these cards in my room…exactly same.'

'So what?' I blinked.

'Give me the last one,' she tried to take it from my hand. I gave her the seventh card:

I just want to spend rest of my life with you…I love you.

'One more is remaining. Wait…'

'Please give it to me, Anuj.'

'No, not so easily, first make sure that you will accept it.' She snatched it and looked at the eighth card:

Will you marry me?

She looked at me, 'How sweet! I love you. Yes, of course. Mamma is coming tomorrow and maybe she'll talk to you about us.'

She added, 'So you made these seven same cards twice, right?'

'I made those cards twice. I gave these to you when we first met and kept one set with myself. When I missed you, I used to read them and fall asleep.

I made the eight one, the last one, recently, which is different and unique.'

'Seriously, madness...you're such a mad lover, no doubt.'

I just smiled and nodded, 'Maybe.'

I shoved my hand into my pocket and kept a box in front of her. She was eager to open it.

'Now what is in it? May I open it?' she asked.

I nodded.

She did, and her lips stretched into a smile.

'Now I have two similar earrings.' She was happy.

'Is it funny?' I asked her.

'Yes, it's funny but the most romantic way to remember the old days and make the present memorable forever. I'm falling in love with you again.'

I gave her one more box to open.

'What is in this?' she asked.

'You can open it,' I said. Removing the gift wrapper from the box, she opened it, 'Oh my God, what the...' She stood up a bit.

'Sit...sit,' I held her hand.

'The same blue and white kurti...the one you gifted me, right?' she looked at me.

'I mean, this is so romantic. I'll go mad with you.' She looked so beautiful and so happy.

'Whatever I made or bought, one for you and one for me, now it's all yours. I think I don't need these anymore because we both are one,' I grinned. 'Now don't be emotional and let's go.'

This was my way of making her remember those promises,

moments and the time we spent together. I was happy that she liked it. We spent some time together and after drawing a beautiful picture full of colours of love and surprises, we left CCD.

We looked around, couples were romancing and waves were touching them as they were in love with them too. Bandstand is Mumbai's famous lovers' point. We were walking on the road together, holding hands. We smiled, looking at each other after looking at those couples.

'What are you thinking?' Pakhi asked, standing in front of me with her long hair, fish-shaped earrings and chubby cheeks.

'Nothing. Let's sit,' I pointed to the place where people were sitting. How sweet life is. At some point of time, life seems over and at another it gives you so much happiness that you wouldn't have dreamt of it. Sometimes it feels like there is no hope but a room with an exit always has an entry. Life is so beautiful if we think about it. The sun rises in the morning and sets in the evening, in between many things happen, some are the best but the rest are not the worst, and they give you experience and make you the real winner in life. Those who have patience and walk on their path reach where they have to reach.

To get everything, you've got to invest something.

Attending an Office Party and Other Dumb Ideas

I was sitting with Pakhi and my phone rang. It was Meera calling. I picked her call and informed her that I met Pakhi.

'You got her address?' Meera enquired eagerly.

'She is sitting in front of me,' I answered simply.

'Give the phone to her. I want to talk to her.' I gave the phone to Pakhi. They talked for a minute or two and then she handed over the phone to me.

'There is a party at office tomorrow, Bansal told me to call and inform you. Come with Pakhi, I've already invited her.'

'Meera, I'm not a part of that company anymore.'

'But the company hasn't cleared your provident fund. You're still a part of this office. By the way, Bansal doesn't ask everyone to come. Stop giving me excuses and join us tomorrow,' she said and I realized that she wanted to meet Pakhi and me. I took some time to reply and was still confused because I didn't want to go there ever again. I realized that Payal would also be there. I paused again for a few seconds.

'Anuj, you're coming, otherwise never talk to me. Let's do one thing. We'll go for shopping at Colaba and then we'll go to the Oberoi hotel for the party. See you tomorrow,' she insisted and disconnected the call.

Now I had the best people in my life: Rahim Chacha, Meera, Anushka and Pakhi. I didn't expect more from this life.

Next day the three of us went to Colaba for shopping. Meera and Pakhi met for the first time but clothes and shopping helped them bond. They bought almost every style of kurti in the market and my hands were full of carry bags.

'It is going to be very tough being a caring husband. How will I manage?' I asked myself a genuine question.

'You'll do everything when she'll come in front of you in a red, lacey nightdress,' my stupid mind replied. As I was lost in weird thoughts, they went and sat on the stools at the mehndi hut. They looked at me, smiled, and said together, 'Just five minutes.'

Applying mehndi to the bride and the groom before the wedding is an old Indian tradition. I wished for that day to come soon and tomorrow was going to be a big day for me as her mother was going to talk to my family. As I had heard from Sharma aunty, the darkness of the colour of the mehndi on a bride's hand represents the deep love and understanding between the bride and her mother-in-law. So I was quite curious to see the colour on her hand.

After their mehndi session, we headed for the party. I was eager to see how dark Pakhi's mehndi would get. After reaching the hotel, they washed their hands and Pakhi's mehndi had turned quite dark and the Rajasthani design looked beautiful on her hands. Meera had applied mehendi for the first time in her life and one could see happiness on her face. They looked like twin sisters.

We entered the party hall. 'Hey, Meera,' said Akshara and waved from the other end. She had joined that company two weeks before I had left.

'Finally you've come,' she added. I nodded and looked around. There were some other girls who I had never interacted with; they were sitting on the sofa in designer dresses and branded glosses on their lips, their silky hair flirting with their cheeks. Everybody was enjoying and why not, it was a party night.

The party had many beautiful, modern girls but I always dreamt of a simple girl with a sweet smile and a cute face...a girl in a punjabi kurti, like Pakhi.

Bansal congratulated me on my new job. I was standing near the bar with Pakhi and everyone met and greeted us.

'One drink,' Meera came to me holding a glass of vodka with orange juice in her hand.

'No, I don't drink,' I said with a smile.

'Just one,' she repeated, looking at Pakhi.

I smiled, 'Thank you.'

'Who are you? No drinks,' she raised her eyebrows.

I nodded, grinned and said, 'I have her, no drinks required.'

Nasha to hum teri aakhon se karte hain,
Hath me pyala to bas ek bahana hai.

She smiled and said, 'I'll just come.' She called Pakhi as well and they both moved to the other side. She looked so hot. Yash, my ex-colleague, came to me and said, 'Meera *kya pataka lag rahi hai, bhai.*'

We were good friends but I never liked it if anyone said anything about Meera. I changed the topic. He was drunk so I expected weird things from him.

'So tell me one thing,' he asked, putting his elbow on the bar counter and holding his drink in his other hand.

'What?' I said.

'What do guys prefer, girls with curves to those without curves like a stick?'

I laughed.

'I'm asking a genuine question, nuts,' Yash always used to do these weird things in parties after two or three drinks of whisky.

'You tell me, what do you like in girls?' I asked and was ready to laugh at him.

'Should I tell you?' he raised his eyebrows.

'Yes, you can,' I was laughing inside.

He started, 'Guys usually like girls with good assets but as far as stick skinny goes—anyone can have big breasts and a decent behind with the help of push-up bras, surgery or the right exercise. Large gives you pleasure and small could mean desperation. Size matters, my friend.'

'But I have a question,' he continued. He seemed to be completely drunk.

'Yes?' I asked as this was stupid but funny.

'Why don't girls in the IT industry have curves? I'm worried about them, how will they make their married life colourful? How will they seduce their hubbies?'

'Don't drink so much and go home. You're already drunk,' I said to him, looking into his red eyes. I went to take a glass of apple juice.

The next moment I saw him, he was holding a microphone and reciting this:

The day starts with a client call and the bloody agenda,
Managers make unachievable objectives and push a big danda.
They call you eat the drop of a hat, for every small issue,
First, they make you cry and then give a big tissue.
Life was like hell without any hope and chances, they said—
Stay late, finish the work, otherwise that will affect your performance.
When this independent country was celebrating Friday,
Those clients raised their issues and made it a dry-day.
Was doing engineering my mistake? I thought for a while.
Money was spent on that, so those programmes I had to compile.
Being a software engineer, I was coding globally
Our nation runs on jugaad that I came to know completely.

Everybody started laughing. Meera came up to me and said, 'Congrats…you got back your love. It rarely happens in reality.'

'Many things happened with me that should not happen in

reality,' I smiled.

'Like?'

'I'll tell you someday. As of now, our families are meeting tomorrow, just pray it goes well.' I was nervous.

My family was not against love marriage but they wouldn't allow me to marry outside the Brahmin caste. Pakhi was from a Maheshwari family so it was going to be a big task to make both the families agree on marriage. 'Oh cool. All the very best and don't forget to send your marriage invitation to me,' Meera said, congratulating Pakhi who was standing next to her. Pakhi looked at me as I had told her that Meera liked me.

We laughed, enjoyed dinner together and left. However, I was thinking about tomorrow.

'Hey, I'm not feeling well,' Pakhi said in a low voice to me.

'What happened?' I asked holding her wrist to measure her pulse as she usually had low blood pressure.

'I don't know, feeling unwell.'

'Let's go…' said Meera.

'Hey listen, Mamaji, Geeta mami, Bhai and Mamma shall reach here in the night. Mama ji has booked rooms in the Trident hotel, so I'll see you tomorrow.' Pakhi said.

'Yes, my family is also reaching tomorrow early morning,' I said and we left.

'May I also come tomorrow to meet these lucky Indian families?' Meera said, teasingly.

Pakhi and I laughed and said together, 'Sure…sure…tomorrow 11.00 a.m.'

When I think about you, I find you around me.
When I remember our days, I smile.
Those moments make me feel like heaven; hope I could hold them forever.

I gave Pakhi a glass of juice and dropped her to her place.

Ready to Take Seven Vows

It was equally exciting for both of us. Though we had known for a while that both the families were going to talk to each other, this was the first time when we were both nervous. Marriage is a huge, serious commitment that shouldn't be taken lightly—when that reality hits you, you end up feeling excited and scared at the same-time. It's totally normal to be a little nervous. We were going to be together forever. Just that thought gave me a sweet shiver. I reminded myself of the seven vows which had started filling more colours in my dreams:

1. The bride and the groom take the first round of the seven vows to pledge that they would provide a prosperous life to the family; that they would look after each other and avoid things that might hinder their healthy living.

2. During the second round of the seven pheras, the bride and groom promise that they would develop their physical, mental and spiritual powers in order to lead a lifestyle that would be healthy.

3. During the third vow, the couple promises to earn an honest living by righteous and proper means, so that their materialistic wealth increases manifold.

4. While taking the fourth vow, the couple pledges to acquire knowledge, happiness and harmony by mutual love, respect, understanding and faith.

5. The fifth vow is taken to continue their heredity by having children, for whom, they will be responsible. They also pray

to be blessed with healthy, honest and brave children.

6. While taking the sixth round around the sacred fire, the bride and groom pray for self-control of the mind, body and soul and longevity of their marital relationship.

7. When the bride and the groom take the seventh and the last vow, they promise that they would be true and loyal to each other and would remain companions and best of friends for life.

I was smiling in my bed at midnight remembering these seven vows of the Hindu marriage that we were supposed to take in the next few weeks.

My cell phone rang. It was Pakhi's mother. 'There must be something she needs before meeting my family,' I thought, still half-asleep.

'Hi, Aunty,' I said, waking up.

'Hey, this is Pakhi's cousin. Di isn't well, so we've come back to Delhi. Mom has said that we can meet after a few days,' she said.

I was worried.

'What happened to her? Tell me everything.' 'She's in the hospital...' she replied. 'She has vomited a lot since this morning but now she's better.'

'Which hospital?' I asked her, urgently. I didn't want to know anything else.

'Indraprastha Apollo hospital.'

I disconnected the call and left for the airport without informing anyone to avoid any kind of delay. It was 2.30 a.m. when I reached and called her again. This time, she picked up.

'What happened to my brave girl?' I got courage as these words came out from my mouth. I had just boarded the flight.

'Don't know why they call me back each time. I know they love me too much but now I don't want to be here. You come here and take me somewhere far away from this place,' she said in a low voice as she was tired. I didn't tell her that I had boarded the flight. She was in the hospital and talked as if she was resting at home and that was the best thing about her that she always tried to be brave, even in awful situations.

The airhostess smiled looking at me and signalled me to switch off my cell phone. I ignored her.

'You just take a nap, I'll be there. I'm on a flight to Delhi,' I replied.

'Seriously?' she said, surprised. This was the third time the airhostess asked me to switch my phone off.

'Flight is ready for take-off, you just take a nap, I'll be there... muahhh. Love you,' I cut the call as I was asked to.

∽

I reached the Indprastha Apollo hospital in a hurry and entered the private ward that her cousin had told me she was in. I found her lying on the bed. The lights were dim. Her mother was sitting on the right side of her bed.

'Oh beta, you have come,' aunty was surprised to see me and stood up. I touched her feet. My eyes fell on the monitor that showed the little blips every time with her heartbeat, there was a 'drip' set up to give her medicines intravenously.

Pakhi slid up and leaned on the wall. 'Think of the devil and the devil is here,' she said in a lazy voice. Her words and expressions showed that she was expecting me.

I came close to her bed, 'Without informing me, you've come here,' I pinched her nose.

The room smelled strongly of a sterile chemical sanitizer. She smiled, her face was dry but still her smile kept up the faith in everyone that she'd be better soon though I wasn't sure she was there. Aunty stood up and sat on the stool. I came and sat where her mother was sitting.

'Beta, you have to take your medicines. Have something,' her mother said to her holding medicines in her hand.

'Ma, I don't want to eat. I'll have after sometime,' she said.

'Aunty, give it to me, I'm also hungry, we will both have some food.' I took the bowl of oatmeal from her mother.

'May I have it first?' I asked her, as she never accepted defeat but it was different from other days. 'Yes, you can,' she replied. She had been staring at me for the last few minutes.

'No, I won't be able to digest it if I have it before you,' I fed her and she ingested a small bite in minutes.

'Nataunki,' she grinned and we both smiled together. Love is all about making each other happy, we knew it very well now as we promised to do it till we breathed our last.

Her mother started doing some cleaning of her tiffin box and folding her clothes with her wet eyes after looking at us. We both finished it together. Then she put her face on my lap and her hands in mine. I felt a drop of water on my hand. I pushed her chin up very gently and felt all the emotions on my hand when she looked with her teary emerald eyes.

'Hey, why these drops in your eyes?' I touched her cheeks and assured myself not to cry with her. I was the weakest person at that time but I had to control myself for her sake.

'Is it possible for you to stay here for a few days?' she gripped my hand tightly like a small kid. I remained silent and let her do whatever gave her comfort.

'I'm here only till the time you don't go back home. Now take rest,' I placed my hands on her cheeks. Her mother was sitting in front of me but at that moment, I didn't care.

She became happy and said, 'Anuj!' She slid herself more close to my lap.

'Yes!' I said, stroking her hair with my hands.

'I'm feeling as if these walls are compressing towards me from all sides. I want to come out and want to walk with you under the open sky as we used to walk together in the rains.'

'What happened?' she asked, shaking my hand slowly.

'Nothing,' I smiled stupidly.

'Tell me...'

I showed her that message from my wallet—Time may be good or bad, I'm always with you. 'Everything is going to be all right.'

Tere bina ek pal nahin jeena, Tere bina mujhe marna nahin,
Tere liye har sapne sanjoye, Tere liye hi har raat bani;
Tune hi mujhko har sapne dikhaye, Tu hi mere liye har gum me hansi,
Tere bina mushkil hai yeh safar, Tere bina koi rah nahin.
Tere bina ek pal nahin jeena, Tere bina mujhe marna nahin,

'Ma, do you really think everything is fine?' Pakhi comfortably compressed herself in bed and asked her mother. Her squinting eyes, her unset hair, white kurti on her body, no earrings in ears as doctor said not to wear any ornaments pushed me into darkness. Her mother came to her bed, put her hand on her forehead and said, 'We lose because we think of losing but we can surely win because you are made for that only. Everything is okay. You just have your medicines, come on,' she took her iPad and kept it on the stool. When I saw her mother last time, she looked younger than her age but now her face was dry, dark circles around her eyes, as she hadn't slept properly since last week.

'She'll have some from me. Pass me those medicines, aunty,' comfortably I released my hand from her to take the medicines.

∽

In the night, the doctor didn't allow many people to stay with her, so I used to be there with her mother and Pakhi forced me to write everything in the diary and she listened to it every night before going to sleep. I started writing each and every moment in that diary. When I missed something, she reminded me to write about it, no matter how romantic and emotional it might be. Whatever time we spent together, I wrote about it in that diary.

It had been more than two weeks and this became a part of

my daily schedule. During the day, I would write and at night I used to narrate the whole story to her.

I slept sitting on the head side of the bed, holding the diary in my hand. I woke up suddenly due to, some unpleasant noise. The clock said 1.30 a.m.

Hanging herself from the bed, she vomited whatever she had eaten in the evening. I held her. She held my hand tightly, 'I'm fine. I need some water. This happened yesterday as well.'

Everyone woke up and her mother gave her some water in a glass. She rubbed her back to make her comfortable from stomach itching.

She took few sips and at the next moment, she vomited again and started vomiting blood.

'Someone call the doctors…' Her mother looked terrified. She ran outside and called everyone.

I was scared and felt a void inside. Her brother ran to call the doctors and her mother took her in her arms, 'Don't worry. My beta is fine.' She started rubbing her head and shoulders while holding her tight in her arms.

'Mom, it's hurting too much. I can't bear the pain…please,' she shouted pressing her chest and stomach.

I was rubbing her feet to keep them warm. Her feet and hands were cold. Her face was changing and tears came in her eyes.

'I don't want to die so soon,' she called me to her bed; she was in tears and looked helpless. She was moaning in pain.

'Nothing will happen.' I kissed her hands.

'Let me call the doctors,' I touched her cheeks with both my hands.

She held my hand, 'You don't go, please.'

Two doctors came with a nurse. One of them kept the oxygen mask on her face and they switched on the cardiac monitor. 'She was groaning and flinching in pain. I went ahead to hold her. Doctors started giving all kinds of drugs through injections, but nothing seemed to relinquish her pain. Other doctor pushed the family out while the nurse closed the door saying, 'Please leave the patient alone.'

Something was wrong. I could see in their expressions. I tried to be there, one doctor took me outside. I pleaded in front of him, 'What happened to her?'

'We are trying our best but this is the last stage, keep faith in God and pray.' He patted on my shoulder and turned.

She was still suffering from the diseases she had mentioned in her email. I had never asked her about it as I didn't want to make her relive those times.

I held his hand, 'Please doctor, please…' He nodded and went inside. Her brother held me. I bent on my knees outside in front of the door and couldn't control my tears. My stomach churned, I felt an aching sensation run through my body and to my head. Everything flashed back. It was excruciating. Her Masi was looking inside from the the glass window at the door. Nothing seemed to comfort me as I sat there numb.

My mom and dad reached the hospital. Mom took aunty away and dad took me. I stood up next to aunty. She hugged me tightly.

'Ma, I'm always here with you. Doctors are trying their best. Everything would be fine.'

After listening to these words from me, she became even more emotional and started crying.

I had called her 'ma' for the first time. The relationship we shared with each other wasn't less than that of a mother and son. I was as sad as her heart but she needed me at that time.

Everyone was waiting outside in pain and everything seemed to have come to a stop.

∽

After two hours, one of the two doctors came and called my dad. Her mother ran towards him, till then he had declared that she was no more with us.

Everyone ran inside. I fell on the floor near the door. Rubbing my hands in pain, I started hitting my head on the wall. I coughed, spattering blood across my body. Dad tried to pick me up. Everything was ruined. All our dreams, promises, a life together—all finished.

'I want to meet her. I need her,' I tried to get up and to reach her bed but wasn't able to. Dad held me. I started shouting.

'Why did this happen to me? Why...' I hit his chest hard.

Dad held me tightly. 'Your dad is always with you.' He broke into tears too.

'Why did this happen to me?' We were going to get married... please I want her back...' I was pleading now, holding his legs, putting my head on his feet.

'Please, dad, I never asked you for anything. Please just call her. I need her back...please,' Dad picked me up. I then turned to my mother because she understood my feelings, 'Mom, you always understand me, at least *you* say something. Please, mom, I won't be able to live...please. I need her...' Nobody was saying anything, just crying.

My elder sister took me inside. Her mother was hugging her body and crying.

Pakhi never made her feel like a widow but after losing her, even the last three-four bangles were no more in her hands.

My mom hugged me and we both cried. Dad held both of us. I held them tightly and sobbed. I wasn't able to see her face. I never wanted to.

'What did you leave...why did you leave?' I cried in pain as I tore away from my parents and went to stand beside Pakhi's bed. 'I faced everything, overruled every difficulty that came for you... why did you then leave me? Why has this happened to me? You can't go. You can't leave like this. Say something...' I again started hitting my head against the bed and then fell to the floor.

I felt someone patted my shoulder and when I opened my eyes, I was on the other bed. When I came to my senses, I saw people taking her body away. The shoulders she used to keep her forehead on to sleep were now taking her bier to the funeral.

In a day, I had lost everything. After the last rites, her remains were collected and tied in a piece of red cloth. The colour she chose for her wedding lehenga. I could still smell the mehndi that she had applied on her hands two days ago, while saying that her mother-in-law loved her so much. I felt ill and empty.

But I couldn't do anything—whatever had to happen had happened. Only tears and pain were left.

Standing near a wall, I held myself against it as I felt an ache run through my soul. It was a strange pain that I had never experienced before. My eyes were sore and burning from all the crying but I just couldn't stop.

As her ashes had to be immersed in flowing water, her family and mine went to Haridwar for her Asthi Visarjan after few days. She flowed into the river but her memories stayed forever in me.

I came to the other side and sat on the secluded bench far from the river.

People, things, nature, everything looked so unstable and worthless. Sitting lonely, I took that note from my wallet and looked at it. I touched those letters and tried to feel them.They said—'Times may be good or bad, I'm always with you.' I could feel her around me but I was brought back to the reality that she was no more with me. I looked at the sky and saw a flying bird that was flying high and high. Someone put a hand on my shoulder. I folded that paper and kept it in my wallet. I turned. Dad came and sat next to me. He handed me a pink coloured note and said, 'Pakhi left something for you. Her mother told me to give it you.'

'What's that?' I snatched it from his hand and opened it. That note said:

Hey listen,

This letter is just to remind you of a few things that you always forget. First stop making these sad faces, I really hate them.

Life is too short to be sad and you can't get it again, so don't cry and listen to what I'm going to tell you.

We promised to be with each other forever and I'm not going to leave you. I think I was the luckiest girl to have met you. We found love in each other and lived but sometimes things aren't in our hands, but that doesn't mean we lost. I'll always be there for you.

By the way, I have told Mamma to find a good girl for you. There is no other piece like me, so it's difficult, but she'll find someone who can love you more than I did. Well, you have enough spark to make her like that;)

I just want you to complete that diary and let people know about us. How's the title? I decided it when you were feeding me yesterday like my hubby.

Your sassy girl

My dad hugged me tightly and said, 'We love someone without any reason but we meet that person for some purpose. Some people come to give a beautiful shape to our lives and she came to yours for the same reason. She had some dreams for you. Go and live for her.'

He held my shoulder and we left.

Epilogue: Few Months Later

Rahim Chacha is no more in this world but his words still motivate me whenever I feel low. Keshav, his son, got a scholarship, and is pursuing an engineering degree from Mumbai University these days. Anushka is now a business analyst and lives in Bengaluru. Navya, my elder cousin, who got married on the day the journey of this book started, is expecting a baby in upcoming months and my hipster cousin Kavya is doing fashion designing from IIFT. Meera is in the US now with her family but she's coming back to India this summer. Payal is married to her boyfriend and now they work together in the same company happily. We talk rarely until she needs any help regarding programming or to resolve any code issues.

One day, as usual, I reached home from office, and my cell phone rang.

'Anuj, when are you coming? It's been more than two months, you haven't come to meet me,' aunty said over the phone. We are very good family friends now. Most of the time, I say silly things to her just to tease her and make her smile. It seems I have two mothers and that makes me feel I'm the luckiest guy on this earth. Sometimes my mother feels jealous when I take advantage of this but they manage with each other. Moreover, I don't know when I started calling her 'ma' but she likes it so I continue to do so. 'I was stuck in some office work, ma, don't worry, will come next weekend, promise. By the way, where is that lady?' I asked her. I was excited to meet her.

'Oh! Your mother…,' she laughed and continued, 'We met just yesterday and she was talking about a girl for you. That girl wasn't bad and is working with an MNC…' I told her, 'Ma, please, not again. Why are you both pestering me like this? Why do you want your kid to become a man so soon?' They both are hunting for a girl for my golden nest as they feel that if I don't find one, one day I'll fly away with someone else who won't care about them but they don't know that I've lost my wings.

'Shut up, sending you the photographs tomorrow. Look at them and let us know,' she said.

'Then say no with a smile. It's too early. By the way, if you find someone extraordinary, let me know.' I teased her and laughed.

'I will find the lucky one for you…'

'Yes, then seven vows, lots of kids and one of them would be named—Pakhi.' Pakhi took a promise from me that I would name my daughter Pakhi.

'Now go and have your dinner, it's quite late.' She seemed sad.

'Ma, don't you love me. I know that,' I tried to make her happy.

'I love you a lot, now go and have your dinner.'

'Love you ma, bye. Good night.'

Whenever she can't resist and misses Pakhi a lot, I call her to Mumbai and we go to Marine drive. However, that golden nest doesn't have anyone but in this journey of two hearts, she gave me the reason to live the way she wanted.

A woman plays a vital role in your life. Not only does she listen to you but also motivates you to achieve your goals, to face problems and resolve difficult issues. If we start describing a girl or woman, we might say many great things about her but can't finish it easily, because words are not enough to describe how great she is. She just needs your love and trust, respect and dedication to be with her forever.

Those who give respect to womanhood, get respect in return, sometimes in the form of love, support and motivation. Moreover, they contribute towards your success.

When you come to your bed after a day of hard work and worries, you need someone to sit next to you. Only a woman is there for you, sometimes in the face of a mother, sometimes as a daughter and sometimes as a wife.

I had one girl who made my existence meaningful and now these mothers who are everything. There is nothing called true or fake love, it's all about how we look at it, how we treat it and what we make of it.

'To be a mother-in-law is the second greatest feeling in the world after giving birth to a girl. I was not as lucky to be his mother-in-law but I became a luckiest mother considering him as my son for rest of my life.'—Abha Maheshwari (Pakhi's mother).

∞

Tu door hai aur pass bhi,
Teri kami hai aur ehsaas bhi.
Jeena chahta hu har lamha tere liye,
Tu zindagi hai aur ek aas bhi.

My mother took out her golden bangles from her old makeup box to gift her the engagement ring. However, there were many questions still troubling my mind. Do people meet again? Do wishes get fulfilled? Everything happens for a reason, I think.

'Success doesn't depend on what your forefathers have done before you, it actually depends on how you take the best from the worst and how you reform the worst as the best.' Dad used to say when we were out for evening walks; nevertheless, somewhere, it touched my heart when life tricked me and I fell. I never cared about those people around me who maligned me. However, people kick only those stones which can roll down.

Different people have different opinions. For some, love is forever and for some it is just a one-night-stand. I had a different opinion—love was my life and it would stay with me till my last breath.

Love makes you weak but it also has the power to make you the winner of the world.

Several people come and go in life, but a few stay forever. Our breath was one from the day our lips touched. We made a golden nest of love full of colours and happiness as we had promised each other. Nevertheless, we can't ignore the immortality of life. If you have something precious, there is always a fear of losing it. Nobody dies for anyone but when someone becomes your need, it becomes difficult to live without them.

There is no word called bad if there is no goodness. Moreover, there is no love if there is no pain.

Spending six months in depression and dying every day in the hospital with her memories, nothing remained in my life; but there was always something around that motivated and inspired me—our promises to live with each other.

Days became awful, especially when doctors told my family to consult a physiologist. Moreover, rumours did their work and I became the topic of evening gossip and an example of some serious mental diseases. I rowed my boat alone and reached the edge. Transcending the Indian society's dramatic barriers of religion and region when it comes to relationships, we did as we had promised each other but God had some other plans.

Acknowledgements

Picking up the pen once again and writing another tale has had some reasons. Before I become more sentimental and go ahead my heartfelt and genuine thanks to all the names I take here, of whom I'll forever be grateful for taking me ahead in the journey of writing this tale of my life.

The most special and adorable readers who loved me so much and supported me, love you all.

Anushka Batra, a crazy 5 feet 2 inches and 59 kg creature and one who can create a spark in ice. She was always ready to do stupid things with me. If I know brands of chocolates, gifts and some girly stuff, it is all thanks to her.

When everyone left my hand, we knocked at many doors in search of Pakhi. Mayank, Ankit and Ankur, thank you for being with me from the day I used to ring your doorbell to go for tuition classes.

Special thanks to Jeeturaaj from Radio Mirchi and the print media who helped me in my journey to find Pakhi and her family. Thanks to my colleagues—Pooja, Tejashree, Surabhi, Apoorva Singh, Abhrekha Jain, Binoy and Vaidehi—for being with me and motivating me.

Meera—born and brought up in Delhi but a US girl. Curvaceous and stunning. She was always there to support me in the vicissitudes of corporate world.

A tribute and salute to Rahim Chacha as he was the best example of humanity. He's no more in this world but his words survive even in his absence.

Love you, mom, dad and di for watching over me always and for listening to me—for the support that went beyond this book. Moreover, thanks to all who unflinchingly gave me their hands to hold.

Thanks to Kapish Mehra and the whole team at Rupa Publications for publishing me and listening to me whenever I flagged queries.

A lot of love to the cities I spent a few years of my life in:

Bareilly: For bringing me up with affection and helping me learn how to be happy with the small things in life.

Lucknow: For always treating me like its own son and giving so much love.

Kanpur: Where I spent a year of my life and learnt about friendship.

Guna: The place that made me an engineer of machines and a narrator of my own life, and for those treasured memories of college days.

Delhi: This place gave me memories to remember for the rest of my life.

Mumbai: Last, but definitely not the least. Mumbai is known as the city people come to to fulfill their dreams, and I know it to be true.